PARAMAAH

THE HIGHEST GOAL

NOBLE J

Contents

Preface

In every arena—be it a roaring stadium or the silent corners of the mind, there is a battle waged not just against opponents, but against doubt, fear, and limitation. *Paramaah – The Highest Goal* is the story of one such challenger. A story that unfolds on the race track but resonates far beyond it.

This is not merely a tale of wins and losses. It is about what drives a person to rise after defeat, to train when no one is watching and to pursue something greater than fame or medal.

"Paramaah" is a Sanskrit word meaning "the highest"—a summit that lies not only in victory, but in purpose, perseverance and self-realization. This book is dedicated to all those who dare to dream big and refuse to settle, who challenge not just the odds but themselves.

Noble Joseph
Author
contact: paramaahthestory@gmail.com

Prologue

Paramaah is the story of a fall and a rise. It is the story of a MotoGP champion who dares to put everything on the line: his body, his pride, his dreams, all for the love of his father, his country, and a goal greater than glory.

Rishab Malhotra's triumph at the World Moto2 Championship marks a defining moment, not just for him, but for every Indian. His win catapults him into the elite circle of global racing legends, securing a coveted spot at the prestigious British MotoGP Championship.

But fate, cruel and unforgiving, has other plans.

A devastating crash robs Rishab of his left leg and with it, his lifelong dream. The accident doesn't just break his body; it fractures his spirit and shatters the once-joyous world around him. His father, Vijay Malhotra, a self-made billionaire and the backbone of the Malhotra legacy succumbs to a heart attack, unable to bear the weight of his son's tragedy.

With Vijay's sudden death, Malhotra Industries falters. The family is thrust into turmoil emotionally and financially. Amidst the chaos, Rishab finds himself abandoned. His closest friends disappear. Even Saira, the woman he loved, walks away. Isolated and broken, Rishab withdraws from the world, consumed by grief and despair. He locks himself away, inching closer to the edge.

But where darkness prevails, sometimes light finds a way in.

Chethana enters his life like a quiet force of nature - gentle, resilient, and unrelenting. She becomes the catalyst that reignites a spark in Rishab's soul. As he embarks on a journey of healing, Rishab crosses paths with people from every walk of life, each one teaching him something vital: about courage, failure, hope, and what it truly means to live.

From shattered dreams rises a new purpose.

In an inspiring turn, Rishab completes the Delhi Half Marathon with a prosthetic leg. Not as a symbol of what he's lost, but of everything he has found.

This is not just a story of motorsports. It is a story of grit, redemption, and the pursuit of something higher than victory—Paramaah, the highest goal.

CHAPTER ONE

THE RAISE

BUDDH INTERNATIONAL CIRCUIT – DAY

It's a picture-perfect day for racing, the sun blazes high in a crystal clear blue sky, casting golden light over the grand stands. The stadium is packed to the brim, a sea of color and energy. The fans from across the globe have gathered, flags waving, chants echoing, cameras flashing. The air is thick with adrenaline. This is the grand finale of the Moto 2 Championship. An atmosphere so charged, you could almost hear the pulse of the crowd.

ON THE TRACK

All eyes are on one man…. Rishab, a two-time National Champion. The crowd's favorite. The pride of a nation, clad in his race suit, he pushes his JMC XTR 500cc motorcycle to the grid. As he reaches his position the stands erupt. "RISHAB! RISHAB! RISHAB!"

His name ripples through the circuit like thunder. He mounts the bike, switches on the ignition, and the engine growls to life. He revs the throttle once, twice and each roar answered by an even louder cheer. But amid the frenzy, Rishab's eyes scan the grandstands, searching….Until he finds her. Saira. smiling through the chaos. Her eyes locked on Rishab.

She blows him a flying kiss and throws a double thumbs-up! her silent, unwavering support. Rishab smiles just for a second and nods back, the fire in his eyes now burning brighter than ever.

In the same section of the stands, his best friends Nikhil, Sid, Ashish and his brother Vivek are all on their feet, screaming his name, waving flags, filled with pride and anticipation.

This isn't just a race. This is Rishab's moment. The victory here means qualification for the British MotoGP Championship — the next big step in his journey.

The engines rev in unison. The lights above the track flash red. The world holds its breath!!

@ THE TRACKSIDE – MOMENTS BEFORE THE RACE

In the second row of the grid stands Vinod, a former National Champion, once the pride of the Indian MotoGP circuit and Rishab's fiercest rival.

He adjusts his gloves, eyes burning with focus. He was 2.6 seconds behind Rishab in the qualifiers, a gap that haunts him, fuels him. Today, he's not here to settle for second.He's here to reclaim glory.

STARTING LINE

Engines rev like thunder rolling across the plains. Twenty riders, One dream. The lights flash red. The crowd holds its breath. The hooter blares and the race explodes into motion.

RACE BEGINS

The riders roar forward, astorm of speed, steel, and fire. Tires screech, engines scream, hearts pound. Within minutes, it's a two-man war at the front — Rishab and Vinod, wheel to wheel, locked in a high-octane duel.

In the first major turn, Vinod slices through like a missile, overtaking Rishab with surgical precision. His technique is flawless, he's dominating the corners, riding with the fury of a man chasing destiny.

For five brutal laps, Vinod commands the race — relentless, confident, and untouchable.

LAP 6 – SECOND CORNER

But then Rishab attacks. He sees the opening, leans hard into the turn, and slews the bike sideways, brushing the very edge of control. With breath-taking finesse he cuts inside and blazes past Vinod, reclaiming the lead.

The crowd goes wild. The JMC pit erupts. From that moment on, Rishab doesn't look back.

FINAL LAP

Every eye is glued to the track. Every heartbeat synced with Rishab's machine. He rockets down the final straight, engine howling, adrenaline peaking and crosses the finish line in style, arms raised in triumph. A new lap time record and a new Champion!!! Rishab wins the Moto 2 World Championship.

VICTORY SCENE

The stadium explodes in celebration with flags waving, fans crying, chants echoing: "RISHAB! RISHAB! RISHAB!"

He coasts the bike to a stop and raises a fist to the sky. Rishab turns to the stands, finds Saira and blows her a kiss.

She can't contain herself. Saira leaps from her seat, rushes past security, and sprints across the track into Rishab's arms. They embrace, a love sealed in victory.

Behind them, Nikhil, Sid, Ashish, and Vivek charge in, all cheering, joy in their eyes as they surround the champ.

ANNOUNCER

"And there you have it, ladies and gentlemen, the undisputed king of Indian MotoGP and now, the new Moto 2 World Champion — RISHAB!!!"

BUDDH CIRCUIT – FINISH LINE – MOMENTS AFTER THE WIN

Bharadwaj, eyes wet and voice choked with pride, leads the JMC racing team in a full sprint down the track. The mechanics, engineers and crew members throw off their headsets and rush to their champion. They reach Rishab and engulf him in a massive group hug. Laughter, tears, high-fives.

Pure jubilation!!!

Bharadwaj pulls Rishab aside and holds him by the shoulders.

BHARADWAJ

"You did it, Champ... You actually did it."

RISHAB

"We did it sir. All of us!!!"

@ THE PODIUM

The crowd roars as Rishab steps onto the top tier of the podium. The cameras flash like lightning, fireworks explode overhead. The Sports Minister of India, Mr.Vikas Jain, steps forward with a beaming smile and hands Rishab:

The Moto 2 Championship Trophy, A gold medal, A symbolic cheque of the grand prize.

The national anthem plays, and Rishab holds the trophy high, his eyes glistening with emotion.

The minister leans in, shakes Rishab's hand firmly, and speaks with a mix of pride and pressure.

VIKAS JAIN

"Well done Rishab !! truly exceptional. I believe we as a country are on the brink of something historic.
The world will be watching next year... Don't let us down.
God bless. Good luck."

RISHAB

(gripping the minister's hand, voice resolute)
"Thank you, sir. I give you my word and will leave no stone unturned. This is more than a race now. It's for my country. For everyone who believed in me. I won't let **INDIA** down."

MUGELLO CIRCUIT, ITALY – LATE AFTERNOON

The golden sun casts long shadows across the famous Mugello track. Alessandro, the reigning MotoGP World Champion, wraps up his practice, holding his helmet in hand, leather suit dusted with grit, he strolls toward the dressing room.

His phone buzzes. A notification lights up the screen.

MotoGP NEWS ALERT:

"RISHAB – New Moto2 Champion. India's Undisputed Racing King Enters the MOTOGP."

Alessandro reads it in silence. A slow smirk spreads across his face.

ALESSANDRO
(muttering in Italian, then English)
"Benvenuto alla corsa... Welcome to the race !!"

He pockets the phone, eyes narrowing with competitive fire and walks off into the shadows of the pit lane.

EMPEROR'S HOTEL, TOKYO – NIGHT

A sprawling luxury suite overlooks the glowing skyline of Tokyo. In the centre of the room, a distinguished man in his 60s, clad in an impeccably tailored suit, stands silently before a massive flat-screen TV. The light from the screen flickers across his composed face. There's pride in his eyes.

On the screen, a news anchor reports with passion:

NEWS ANCHOR

"Rishab – a true champion, both on the track and in life. Born into one of India's most successful business families, he's never relied on legacy. Instead, he's rewritten his own story — one race at a time."

CUT TO TV – MONTAGE:

Footage plays of Rishab on the track, his helmet off, arms raised in triumph. Another shot: Him speaking at a business conference. Then: Working with his race crew, laughing with fans, and racing past the checkered flag.

NEWS ANCHOR

(continuing)

"An automobile engineer and an MBA from Stanford Business School, Rishab serves as the Vice President of Malhotra Industries, where he's been instrumental in driving growth across the Asia-Pacific market.
But despite his towering business success, it's the race track where his soul truly comes alive."

The man watching Vijay Malhotra, founder of Malhotra Industries smiles faintly, his hand resting lightly on the TV stand. His usually stern face softens.

NEWS ANCHOR(V.O.)

"Rishab's father, Vijay Malhotra , a self-made titan of Indian manufacturing industry has long been his guiding star. A man who didn't just build an empire, but fuelled a dream. A father who didn't clip wings, but taught his son how to fly."

Vijay turns off the TV. He stands in silence. Then, barely a whisper...

VIJAY

"You made your own name, son... and now, the world knows it!!!"

He walks to the window, looks out at the Tokyo skyline, his reflection barely visible in the glass.

VIJAY (CONT'D)

"And I've never been prouder..."

VINTAGE HOTEL – AFTER RACE PARTY

The ballroom is alive. A dazzling mix of celebration, champagne, and flashbulbs. The racers, officials, and sponsors mingle under golden chandeliers, the media swarms, cameras flashing, microphones stretching for soundbites.

At the centre of it all: Rishab, surrounded by reporters and fans, every eye drawn to the man of the moment. He smiles, graciously acknowledging praise, offering quotes with charm and humility.

Suddenly, VIVEK pushes through the crowd, phone in hand, his face lit with emotion.

VIVEK

"Bro... Papa's on the line."

Rishab's smile freezes. A flash of emotion washes over him. He nods quickly and excuses himself from the press. He grabs the phone.

RISHAB

(breathless, voice trembling slightly)

"Papa... I did it. I won the championship."

EMPEROR'S HOTEL, TOKYO

Vijay Malhotra stands by the window of his opulent suite, city lights glowing behind him. He holds the phone to his ear, his usually commanding voice now soft, full of pride.

VIJAY

(with warmth, and gentleness)

"Congratulations, Son. You're one step closer to your dream. You've made the country proud... and you've made me proud."

INTERCUT BETWEEN RISHAB & VIJAY

Rishab's eyes brim with emotion as he listens, the noise of the party fading into the background.

RISHAB

"Thank you, Papa...I just wish you were here."

A pause.

VIJAY

(with quiet regret)

"So do I. It breaks my heart not to be standing beside you tonight. I'll be on the first flight out to Delhi tomorrow. We'll meet Sunday morning and that's a promise."

RISHAB

(smiling through the emotion)

"Safe journey, Papa."

VIJAY

"Thank you, Son. Now go... soak in your moment. You earned every second of it."

The call ends. For a moment, Rishab just stands still, letting the weight of it all settle.

The music swells and Rishab standing tall in the middle of a crowd not just a champion of the track, but a son, a dreamer, and now... a symbol of hope and success.

VINTAGE HOTEL

The party is beginning to wind down. Bharadwaj approaches Rishab, his eyes filled with pride but also the weight of what lies ahead.

BHARADWAJ

"Rishab... the first milestone is behind us and now comes the real climb. We will regroup in one month. I have a meeting with the association next week, will push hard to get the best international coach for you. No compromises. We train like the title depends on it... because it does.!"

RISHAB
(nods firmly)
"Yes, sir. Thank you !!"
They share a handshake not just one of professionalism, but of deep mutual respect. A silent understanding passes between them.

After bidding farewell to Bharadwaj and the team, Rishab weaves through the party crowd, searching the room until he spots them — his gang. Nikhil, Sid, Ashish, and Vivek sit around a corner table, laughing over drinks.

Saira standing by the window, her eyes scanning the crowd below with quiet intensity.

RISHAB
(raising a brow, playful but urgent)
"Alright, champions — let's roll. I've got a surprise planned for mom and need to be home before dinner or risk being disowned."

They laugh, clink their glasses one last time, and rise. The men leave the room, giving Rishab and Saira their space.

Rishab comes close to his lady love. The energy of the race day finally giving way to something gentler, more intimate. They face each other and are very close.

SAIRA
(smiling softly)
"You should get going. Your mom's waiting."

RISHAB
(nods, reluctantly)
"Yeah... she'll pretend she's mad that I'm late, but I know she's been praying all day."

SAIRA
"That's how mothers are. They worry... even when we win."

RISHAB
(looking into her eyes)
"Thank you for being there today—you gave me a strength
you may never realize"

They both laugh softly. Then, silence — the kind that
speaks.

RISHAB
(takes a step closer)
"I've to go now... but I'll see you tomorrow morning...I
promise."

SAIRA
"You better. Don't make me come drag you out of that
training camp."

RISHAB
(deeply sincere)
"Nothing will keep me away from you."

He leans in and kisses her, a lingering heartfelt gesture.
Her eyes close as she absorbs the moment. Rishab turns
and walks toward his car. Saira stays by the gate, watching
him until he disappears down the street.

HIGHWAY – NIGHT

Rishab and Vivek are in the car, headlights cutting
through the darkness as they race toward Delhi. The city
glows faintly in the distance. Rishab had also made sure
Saira and the rest of the group got home safely. But now, his
mind is elsewhere — on the one woman who hadn't seen a
single second of his victory.

MALHOTRA HOME – LIVING ROOM

Sujatha, Rishab's mother, sits alone in the dimly lit
room, a prayer lamp flickering softly beside her. Her eyes
are closed, lips murmuring a quiet prayer.

She hadn't watched the race. She never does, not
because she doesn't care, but because every rev of her son's

engine tears through her soul.

She clutches the edge of a shawl as she thinks of Vivek, her younger son. A medical student - disciplined, focused boy, yet lately his interest leaning towards motorcycle racing.

Her greatest pride... and her deepest fear.

The doorbell rings, echoing through the quiet house. Sujatha opens the door and finds Rishab standing there, grinning ear to ear, still in his racing suit, clutching the massive Moto 2 GP trophy. Before she can say a word, he lunges forward, wrapping her in a tight embrace.

RISHAB

(excited, breathless)

"Maa! Your son is the new Moto 2 GP Champion!"

SUJATHA

(tears in her eyes, smiles softly)

"Congratulations, My dear.."

RISHAB

(bursting with pride)

"Maa, I've qualified for the British Moto GP Championship
in London! It's the biggest race in the world, the real
battlefield, top machines, top racers... It's going to be war."

For a moment, Sujatha smiles, overwhelmed, but her expression shifts. The gleam in her eyes dims. She turns away without a word and quietly walks toward the dining table, beginning to lay out plates in silence.

Rishab watches, the weight of her silence falling hard on his chest. He follows her.

RISHAB

(softly)

"Maa... you know this isn't just a race for me. This is my
life. My dream. Representing India at the World
Championship... that's what I've fought for every single

day."
SUJATHA
(still not looking at him)
"And every race you ride, I sit here with my heart in my throat, praying nothing goes wrong.
Now you're flying across the world to risk everything again..."
She finally turns, eyes moist, voice low but heavy.
SUJATHA
(bitterly)
"You call it a dream, I call it a nightmare that I have to live through again and again. I'm your mother, Rishab. I want to be proud of you and not terrified for you."

There's a heavy silence. Rishab stands still, the trophy suddenly heavier in his hands. His excitement fades into quiet heartbreak. Without a word, he turns and walks slowly toward his room, the silence between them louder than any cheer from the crowd.

Vivek, standing by the kitchen watches the exchange unfold. He steps forward, trying to break the tension.
VIVEK
(half-heartedly, trying to cheer her)
"Maa... come on. He made history today."
SUJATHA
(quietly)
"Yes... but at what cost?"

She walks back into the kitchen, wiping a single tear from her cheek.

TAJ MAHAL HOTEL – SUCCESS PARTY - SATURDAY NIGHT

The grand ballroom of the iconic Taj Mahal Palace is alive with music, laughter, and clinking glasses. The ambient lights shimmer over the dance floor as Rishab's close friends Ashish, Nikhil, Sid, and a few familiar faces from the racing world raise their glasses in celebration. At the heart of it all is Rishab, glowing with pride.

Saira, radiant and elegant, stands by his side — his most special guest for the evening.

A large cake bearing the inscription "Moto 2 World Champion" is wheeled in. The crowd gathers, phones out, flashes blinking.

RISHAB
(grinning wide)
"To victory, to passion, and to all of you who believed in me!"

He cuts the cake, takes the first piece, and gently feeds it to Saira. She smiles, eyes misty, and hugs him tightly. The two kiss igniting cheers from the crowd.

The champagne cork pops and Rishab raises the glass high. The music swells and the room erupts into a whirl of celebration dancing, laughter, memories in the making.

Rishab steps away for a moment to grab his drink from the bar and as he turns around, he spots Vinod across the ballroom. He is with his family, seated at a private table. Rishab walks over with a warm smile.

RISHAB
(graciously)
"Hey Vinod. Good to see you, man. You should join us, come celebrate."

VINOD
(cool, dismissive)
"No thanks. I'm with my family."

RISHAB

(nods, still smiling)

"Alright. Enjoy the evening."

Rishab turns to walk away, but Vinod's voice stops him mid-step.

VINOD

(raised voice, oozing arrogance)

"You got lucky, Rishab. My throttle jammed at turn 14. Otherwise, I would've crossed that finish line first."

Rishab turns back. The party sound fades just slightly as the two racers lock eyes. The air tightens.

RISHAB

(calm, sharp)

"Vinod, you weren't close but 1.8 seconds behind. In our world, that's a lifetime."

He walks step closer, eyes steady.

RISHAB

"And yes, you're right about one thing. The luck does favour some of us, but only when we bleed for our dreams. Try harder next time mate."

Rishab flashes a charming smile, turns and walks back into the glow of his party, his arm slipping around Saira. Vinod watches him go - stiff, shoulders tense, applause ringing behind him like a reminder of everything he lost.

The music swells again. Rishab and his friends raise their glasses.The celebration roars back to life. The champagne flows, laughter echoes, and Rishab the people's champion dances into the night, a man who has earned every cheer.

***

MALHOTRA HOME – SUNDAY MORNING

The doorbell rings. Sujatha, still in her kitchen apron, wipes her hands quickly and rushes to the door. She opens it to seeVijay Malhotra, suitcase in hand, standing tall and smiling after a long business trip.

SUJATHA

(beaming)

"Very good morning, my dear!"

She throws her arms around him. They share a warm embrace, the kind that holds years of love.

VIJAY

(chuckling softly)

"Good morning, Sujatha."

She takes his bag and leads him inside with affection.

SUJATHA

(while walking)

"Hope the flight was good? You look a little thinner though..."

VIJAY

(teasing)

"I missed your food. Even five-star chefs can't match your magic."

SUJATHA

(smiling)

"Breakfast will be ready by the time you freshen up."

VIJAY

(looking around)

"Is Rishab still asleep?"

SUJATHA

"He got home at 3 AM. The party went late."

RISHAB'S BEDROOM – MOMENTS LATER

Vijay quietly pushes the door open. Rishab is fast asleep, still in his post-party fatigue. Vijay walks over, sits beside him and gently touches his forehead. His eyes drift to the trophy on the shelf, gleaming under the morning light. He walks to it.

INSCRIPTION:
RISHAB MALHOTRA
Winner – Moto 2 World Championship – 2023

Beside it are dozens of medals, certificates, and shining trophies — the legacy of a racer who never gave up. Vijay runs his fingers across the championship trophy, emotion swelling in his eyes. A proud smile forms. His son has truly made history.

DINING HALL – MOMENTS LATER

Sujatha calls out while setting the table.

SUJATHA

"Breakfast is ready! Vijay, Vivek, come on!"

Vijay enters, brushing his hair. Vivek, energetic and cheerful, joins him.

VIVEK

(hugging him)

"Good morning, Papa! How was the Tokyo trip ?"

VIJAY

"It was good. But tell me, didn't you join your brother's celebration last night?"

VIVEK

(disappointed)

"He never takes me. Says I'm still in training mode."

VIJAY

(grinning, to Sujatha)

"You'll have two racers in the house at this rate."

SUJATHA

(teasing)

"God help me if that happens."

VIJAY

(softly, smiling)

"There's good news. Let's wait until lunch.. I want Rishab to hear it too."

DRAWING ROOM – AFTERNOON

Vijay is working on his laptop, while Vivek watches cricket on TV.

VIJAY

"Son, please lower the volume."

Vivek grabs the TV remote. Just then, Rishab walks in, freshly showered, hair tousled, still glowing from his triumph. He sees his father and runs over, hugging him tight.

RISHAB

"Papa!"

VIJAY

(hugging back, with pride)

"Congratulations, champ. You did it. You made all of us proud. Hope you had a blast last night."

RISHAB

"Thanks, Papa! Last night was magical."

VIJAY

(grinning)

"I have some big news."

RISHAB

(getting curious)

"Wait, what is JMC saying ?"

VIJAY

"They've officially approved your engine and gearbox enhancements. Their R&D team loved the torque, fuel efficiency and the compact engine design."

RISHAB

(stunned)

"What?! Are you serious?"

VIJAY

(smiling wide)

"They want us to build engines for their 250cc motorcycle

segment. We've landed the contract."

Rishab jumps in the air with a loud cheer. The sound thunders through the house.

SUJATHA

(from the kitchen, alarmed)

"What's going on?"

She rushes in. Rishab turns to her, unable to contain his joy.

RISHAB

"Maa! We're building engines for JMC!"

VIJAY

"Their top executives will be in Delhi on the 21st of May.

Two weeks from now. We've got work to do."

RISHAB

(eyes gleaming)

"Leave it to me, Papa. I'll handle everything."

The family sits together, joy written on every face. Laughter fills the air. The champion has returned, and a new journey has just begun.

For nearly two years, Rishab and his team ofengineers have been dedicated to developing a robust and high-performance engine and gearbox for one of their most prestigious clients — **Japan Motor Company (JMC).**

JMC is a market leader in Asia for 100cc and 250cc motorcycles and securing this contract marks a significant milestone for Malhotra Industries Limited (MIL). It opens the doors to a strategic partnership with the Japanese automotive giant. A game-changing opportunity for the company.

MALHOTRA INDUSTRIES – THE BIG DAY.

It's a landmark morning at Malhotra Industries Limited (MIL). The prestigious delegation from JMC is arriving to sign a contract that could propel MIL into the international spotlight.

The atmosphere is electric. The entire facility is dressed to impress , vibrant floral arrangements adorn the hallways, the offices gleam with polish and even the buzzing production floor seems to hum with anticipation. Every detail has been considered, nothing has been left to chance.

The plan is meticulous: a full tour of MIL's production units, the state-of-the-art R&D lab, and the operations command centre. The staff has been instructed to arrive early, dressed immaculately. The technicians have been explicitly reminded to wear their full safety gear. The management wants to show- case a world class working environment at MIL to the Japanese executives.

Rishab arrives early to office. His eyes scan every corner, his mind ticking through a mental checklist. Everything must be perfect, until he finds a technician in barefoot but a pair of worn out slippers standing in the production floor.

Rishab's expression hardens. He storms across the floor with anger.

RISHAB

(angrily)

"Anand! Where the hell is the discipline? Didn't I make myself crystal clear last week? No exceptions. No compromises. So tell me why is this man out here without his safety shoes?"

Anand, the Production Supervisor rushes over, flustered and pale.

ANAND

"Sir, Gupta injured his foot last week. A deep cut. The

doctor's orders were strict, no enclosed footwear until it heals."

Rishab's face twists, torn between frustration and disbelief. His voice drops, cold and sharp.

RISHAB

"Then why is he even here? What part of "safety first" is so hard to understand?"

He turns to Gupta, eyes blazing.

RISHAB

(firm, but intense)

"Gupta, you've been one of our finest but this? This is negligence and will cost us dearly in front of our partners.

Go home, come back only when you're fit to follow protocol. I want you out of this building in the next five minutes."

The production floor falls silent. Gupta, the most senior machinist, lowers his head. His eyes glisten with humiliation. Wordless, he walks away with each step echoing louder than the last, past his stunned colleagues who can barely meet his gaze.

Rishab watches him go as the weight of leadership sinks in.

MALHOTRA INDUSTRIES – RECEPTION

The JMC executives are welcomed with grandeur and warmth by Rishab, Vijay and the entire MIL staff. A traditional welcome, complete with flowers and folded hands blends seamlessly with corporate decorum. Smiles, handshakes, respectful bows , it is more than hospitality; it is history in the making.

MIL – BOARDROOM – CONTINUOUS

The atmosphere is electric, walls lined with legacy photographs silently witness the unfolding milestone. Rishab and Vijay escort the JMC team to their seats, flanked by MIL's board of directors. The contracts are signed between the partners. The final handshake seals it.

A historic alliance. A moment that echoes through the journey of a company that began as a humble workshop 35 years ago — now partnering with a global giant JMC.

A quiet, proud gleam flashes in Rishab's eyes. Vijay blinks away the emotion behind his calm demeanour.

MIL – PRODUCTION FLOOR, R&D LAB, MANUFACTURING UNITS

The tour begins. The visiting executives walk through buzzing production lines, cutting-edge lab and the assembly units. Everywhere they look, excellence stares back.

The JMC team nods, impressed. The transformation of MIL is undeniable.

MIL – CONFERENCE HALL – EVENING

A large gathering of MIL staff waits. The murmurs quiet as Haruto Ki, the charismatic CEO of JMC, steps up to the podium. He pauses, looks around, then speaks - calm, assured, powerful.

HARUTO KI

(voice firm, eyes kind)

"Today marks not just a partnership between two companies, but the beginning of something far greater — a shared future."

The crowd listens, captivated.

HARUTO KI (CONT'D)

"We see in Malhotra Industries not just capability but character. Passion. Vision. It is our honour to walk alongside you."

He smiles, then drops the announcement that sends a ripple through the room.

HARUTO KI (CONT'D)

"Ladies & Gentlemen, now I have a BIG announcement. We are proud to share that Rishab Malhotra will be riding the JMC-XTR 1000 at next year's British MotoGP in London."

Hearing the announcement the crowd bursts into thunderous applause. The staff members leap to their feet, clapping, cheering. The pride is visible on every face. Rishab smiles — humbled, honoured. He nods at Haruto, then to his team & his family.

CONVENTION HALL – MIL CAMPUS – EVENING

Vijay Malhotra hosts a grand celebration, a night to remember for family, friends, MIL staff and the JMC executives. Lush floral arrangements, golden chandeliers, and a lavish spread of Indian cuisine line the venue. The aroma of spices, the clink of glasses and the warmth of shared success create a vibrant symphony of joy.

Saira stands with her parents Mr and Mrs. Rastogi, esteemed physicians in the city. She looks graceful, radiant, quietly observing the jubilant energy around her.

On the main stage, Vijay Malhotra and Haruto Ki stand beside a towering celebration cake. The flashbulbs pop as they cut it together, a symbol of a partnership sealed in trust and ambition. The room lifts their glasses in a grand toast as cheers and applause ringing across the hall.

The music plays and the dance floor springs to life.

Suddenly — the rhythm halts.

All heads turn as Rishab steps up to the DJ console and picks the mic. The lights dim slightly, focusing on him.

RISHAB

(easy, steady voice)

"Good evening, Ladies and Gentlemen. I hope you're all having a wonderful evening. Today has been special in so many ways... but for me, it's about to become unforgettable."

He steps away from the console, walking deliberately and now everybody's eyes fixed on him. He moves toward Saira, seated with her parents, her expression changing from surprise to awe.

Rishab stops in front of her. Slowly, reverently, he drops to one knee. A velvet box appears in his hand, a sparkling diamond ring . The entire hall holds its breath.

RISHAB

(soft, emotional)

"Saira, from the first time I saw you, I knew you were the one. You've stood by me, believed in me through storms and triumphs. Tonight, in front of everyone I want to ask, Will you marry me?"

The silence is broken by the soft gasp of Saira — eyes brimming, lips trembling.

SAIRA

(overwhelmed, joyful)

"Yes... yes, Rishab!"

The room erupts in cheer, applause, laughter. Some wipe away tears. A crescendo of happiness fills the hall.

Rishab rises, and they embrace, a kiss sealing not just a proposal, but a promise. Vijay and Sujatha step forward, eyes shining with pride, and wrap the couple in a warm embrace.

VIJAY

(to Saira)

"Welcome to the family, dear!!"

Mr & Mrs. Rastogi join in, heartfelt and emotional, blessing the couple. It was more than a celebration of business success but also the coming together of two hearts, two families and the beginning of a new chapter.

RISHAB'S BEDROOM – MORNING

Dressed in workout gear, Rishab laces his shoes, headphones slung around his neck, about to leave for the gym. A gentle knock at the door.

RISHAB

(looking up)

"Come in."

The door opens. Vijay Malhotra steps in, his face calm but weighed down by something unspoken.

RISHAB

(smiling)

"Good morning, Papa."

VIJAY

(softly)

"Good morning, Son. Can we talk once you're back from the gym?"

Rishab senses the gravity in his father's tone. He straightens, concern flickering across his face.

RISHAB

"If it's serious, we can talk now."

VIJAY

(heavy voice, measured)

"Yes... it is. Very serious."

There's a beat of silence. Rishab's expression tightens.

RISHAB

(worried)

"Is everything okay Papa? Did something go wrong yesterday?"

VIJAY

(sighs, with quiet disappointment)

"It's about the incident on the shop floor yesterday

morning."
Rishab's tone shifts , cautious, a little defensive.
RISHAB
(firmly)
"What about it?"
VIJAY
"You know what happened. Guptaji is not just a senior employee, he's been the heart and soul of this company for over 30 years. He has poured his sweat and blood into building this organization, often putting it before himself. Whatever we are today is because of the unwavering dedication, hard work and sacrifices of people like him."
RISHAB
(unhappy, defensive tone)
"Papa, I was only trying to ensure we maintained compliance especially with our partners watching.
You know better than anyone how particular the Japanese are about discipline and standards. I couldn't afford a single slip-up."
Rishab nodding his head in disbelief...
RISHAB
(continues)
"Well, speaking of their blood and sweat, the employees work hard and we ensure they receive their rightful due. Our compensation and perks are among the best in the industry."
VIJAY
(Angry tone)
"Stop it Rishab !! I've always considered the employees of MIL as my extended family. They're not just workers, they're the backbone of everything we've built. They're getting what they truly deserve, and let me be clear: we're not doing them any favour by giving them their due. I

started with a small lathe factory right here in this city. In those difficult early days, it was Guptaji who stood by me. He and a handful of others worked day and night, shoulder to shoulder, never once complaining. I'll never forget how, when your mother's health took a turn while she was pregnant with your brother, it was Guptaji's wife who stepped in and nursed you like her own child. That's the kind of bond we share, it's not just about business, it's about loyalty, sacrifice, and family."

Few seconds of slience.

VIJAY

(continues)

"If I'm not here tomorrow, I trust that my children will carry this legacy forward, treating our employees like family and always standing by them."

An emotional Vijay walks up to Rishab, places a firm yet gentle hand on his son's shoulder, and speaks in a quiet, heartfelt voice...

VIJAY

"I believe in you, son... and I know you won't let me down."

Rishab does not react and quietly leaves. Vijay continues to stand and watch his son exit the room. Rishab does not regret and still believes that whatever he did is right and in the company's interest.

MALHOTRA INDUSTRIES – CAFETERIA

Rishab and his team of design engineers walk into the cafeteria, the hum of casual chatter and the aroma of coffee filling the air. His eyes scan the room and lands on Gupta, seated at a corner table, sipping coffee with a few of his colleagues.

As they pass, Gupta catches Rishab glancing down at his feet. It wasn't a casual look. Rishab was checking whether the old man is wearing his safety shoes, as required on the shop floor.

Noticing the scrutiny, Gupta offered a gentle smile, a quiet gesture of acknowledgment, but Rishab didn't return it. He simply turned away and re-joined his team, his expression unreadable.

MONTAGE:

Rishab is racing against time. By day he's building the Infrastructure for JMC's engine and gearbox manufacturing unit; by night, he roars on the racetrack, training relentlessly for the World MotoGP championship under the supervision of Bharadwaj.

METRO RACE ACADEMY – LATE EVENING.

Rishab had been pushing the limits on the JMC XTR 1000, every lap on the track sharpening his instincts and testing the machine's edge. As the sun dipped lower, casting long shadows across the asphalt, he guided the bike into the pit lane.

He hands the motorcycle over to the training team with a nod, sweat clinging to his brow, his mind still replaying every turn and throttle. He turned and began walking toward the dressing room,

Just then, Bharadwaj's voice rang out behind him.

Rishabturns around, with the helmet tucked under his arm and removing the gloves

BHARADWAJ

"Good news! David Reynolds is going to be your coach for the MotoGP boot camp. He's flying into Chennai in the last week of this month. Please get ready for some serious

next-level training!"
RISHAB
(ecstasy)
"That is great news !!"
BHARADWAJ
"David wants to kick off the boot camp at the start of next month. The association is pulling out all the stops to back you — no compromises. From what I hear... even the Sports Ministry is watching this closely."
He pauses, letting the weight of that sentence sink in.
BHARADWAJ
(CONT'D)
"The Madras Racing Academy (MRA) tracks are being tuned to perfection. You'll have a full dossier in your inbox by tomorrow morning , the schedule, crew assignments, everything."
RISHAB
(sharp, focused)
"I can't wait to hit that track. MRA feels like home turf. Thank you so much sir !!"
Bharadwaj nods with a smile.

As Rishab turns to leave, the mood shifts. He walks toward the dressing room, the weight of expectation trailing behind him.

David Reynolds, a name that echoes through MotoGP history. A former rider turned legendary coach, he's carved champions out of raw talent in the MotoAmerica AMA and the FIM North American Road Racing circuits. Now, he brings that legacy to Team India and to Rishab Malhotra.

MALHOTRA HOME – DINING ROOM – NIGHT
The family sits around the large dining table. The atmosphere is warm, yet something lingers beneath the surface tension, unspoken concern. The clinking of cutlery

is the only sound for a moment.

RISHAB

(casually, but with excitement)

"Papa... my boot camp starts on the first day of next month. I'll be training under David Reynolds. The first schedule runs for 20 days."

VIJAY

(sincerely, with pride)

"That's excellent. You're lucky, Rishab. David Reynolds is the best in the business."

Just then, Sujatha quietly places her fork down, her appetite lost. Without a word, she rises from the table and walks away toward the kitchen, leaving her plate half-finished. Vijay watches her go. He looks at Rishab and speaks softly, almost like a father handing down wisdom.

VIJAY

(convincing, understanding)

"Go to her. She needs to hear it from you."

Rishab nods, his heart heavy. He rises and walks slowly into the kitchen.

KITCHEN – CONTINUOUS

Sujatha stands by the sink, her back turned, staring blankly out the window. Rishab approaches gently, wraps his arms around her from behind.

RISHAB

(softly, filled with emotion)

"Maa... how can I give my best out there when I know you're hurting in here? Seeing you like this — sad and worried, it tears me apart."

Sujatha says nothing for a moment, her shoulders trembling slightly, then in a soft voice.

SUJATHA

(teary)
"I'm your mother, Rishab. How can I not worry? This racing... it's not just a sport. It's risk."
Rishab gently turns her around and takes her hands in his.

RISHAB
(earnest, emotional)
"I know, Maa. I feel your fear and love every time I put on that helmet. But this dream... it's not just mine anymore. It's for our family. Our country. No Indian has ever gone this far in MotoGP. I want to carry our flag to the world stage."

SUJATHA
(eyes welling, voice breaking)
"You've come so far... I just want you to come back safe."

RISHAB
(smiling through the emotion)
"I promise I will. But I need you with me , your blessings, your smile, your belief. That's what fuels me, Maa.
Without that... even the best bike in the world can't take me across the finish line."
She breaks and pulls him into a tight, emotional hug. A mother's surrender.

DINING ROOM – MOMENTS LATER
Rishab returns to the table. Vijay is still seated, sipping water, waiting patiently. Rishab sits beside him, the earlier tension now softened.

RISHAB
(focused, serious)
"Papa... I'm worried about the JMC project in my absence."

VIJAY
(reassuring)
"Don't worry, Rishab. I'll personally oversee the execution

while you're at camp. You just focus on the training and give it everything you've got."

RISHAB

(nods)

"I'll still attend the project review calls remotely. The plan and client presentation are nearly 75 percent done. I will finalize everything in the next couple of days."

VIJAY

(supportive, with a smile)

"Sure, son. I know you will."

TAJ HOTEL –SUNDAY EVENING

Soft lighting. Laughter. The clinking of glasses. The restaurant glows under the setting sun as Rishab hosts a warm, intimate dinner for his closest friends and Saira.

NIKHIL

(grinning, raising his glass)

"Bro... we're so damn proud of you."

SID

"Seriously, man. Training under David Reynolds? That's legendary."

RISHAB

(nods, humble but excited)

"It's going to be intense, toughest challenge of my life so far."

ASHISH

(grinning)

"So... are we allowed to crash your boot camp on weekends?"

RISHAB

(laughs)

"I don't see why not. As long as you don't get me into

trouble."

The group laughs but Rishab's eyes drift toward Saira, who sits quietly, stirring her drink, lost in thought. He leans in gently and places his hand over hers.

RISHAB (softly)

"Hey... what's going on? You've been quiet all evening."

Before Saira can speak, Ashish pipes up with a teasing grin.

ASHISH

(smirking)

"Hope you are not taking Saira with you to Chennai?"

SAIRA

(irritated, low)

"Shut up, Ashish."

A moment of silence. The mood softens. Rishab doesn't let go of her hand.

TAJ HOTEL PARKING – LATE EVENING

The dinner is over and friends share hugs and handshakes. Nikhil, Sid, and Ashish wish Rishab good luck and promise to visit. But Saira lingers. She stands by Rishab's bike, unwilling to let the night or him go just yet. The wind rustles gently through the trees.

RISHAB

(quietly, with a half-smile)

"It's a beautiful night... Wanna go for a ride?"

SAIRA

(small smile, eyes glistening)

"Yes."

❧❧❧

CITY STREETS / HIGHWAY – NIGHT

Rishab and Saira cut through the city on his XTR 1000RR. The world blurs around them as the bike roars onto the open highway. Saira holds him tight, her arms wrapped around his waist. The tension of the evening melts into the wind. Above them, stars shimmer in the velvet sky. The moon spills silver across the road ahead.

A soft **drizzle** begins light, playful as though the night itself is blessing their bond.

Saira's hair dances in the wind and she leans in closer, her head resting lightly on Rishab's back. It was just two hearts chasing dreams on a road that felt endless... and entirely their own.

SAIRA'S HOME - LATE NIGHT.

After a deeply romantic ride, Rishab pulls up in front of Saira's home. The night air feels charged with the moments they've shared. They linger for a moment, their hands still clasped as they exchange a soft hug and a tender kiss, reluctant to say goodbye.

SAIRA

(her voice barely a whisper, full of emotion)

"All the best for your boot camp."

Saira begins walking toward the gate, but then something pulls at her heart. She turns abruptly, her feet carrying her back to Rishab. She wraps her arms around him tightly, as if trying to hold on to the moment, and plants a gentle, lingering kiss on his cheek.

SAIRA

(with a quiet intensity)

"This ride... this moment... will always remain in my heart.

I love you."

RISHAB

(his voice thick with emotion, holding her close)

"Love you too !!"

After bidding Saira goodbye, Rishab speeds back home, his mind racing as he realizes he still hasn't packed for his early morning flight to Chennai.

The late evening drizzle has turned into a downpour, with rain pounding down heavily, the fog quickly begins to settle on his face shield making it increasingly difficult for Rishab to see clearly.

CHAPTER TWO

THE FALL

Rishab crosses a signal and takes a sharp right turn at high speed, only to find an SUV coming straight at him from the opposite direction. He doesn't have enough time to reduce his speed and loses grip. The bike collides head-on with the SUV.

The impact is brutal and Rishab is flung into the air, landing hard on the road with his left leg hitting first.

He lies motionless on the pavement, unconscious. The driver doesn't even bother to stop and speeds away, with a broken bumper.

It's only two hours later that a passing taxi driver notices Rishab lying in a pool of blood. He stops and without hesitation, rushes him to the hospital in his taxi.

VIJAY'S BEDROOM – MIDNIGHT.

Vijay is busy reviewing the JMC project plan on his laptop. He looks at the clock and stretches himself.

VIJAY

"Sujatha?"

SUJATHA

(sleeping, mumbles)

"Hmm..."

VIJAY

(Bothered)

"Rishab still isn't home, and he has a morning flight."

SUJATHA

(Suddenly waking up, rubbing her eyes)

"Sorry... I must've dozed off. Let me call him."

Just then, Vijay's mobile phone rings. He glances at the screen and notices an unknown number. His fingers hesitate for a moment before he answers.

THE VOICE

(sharp and urgent, from the other end of the phone)

"Am I speaking to Mr. Vijay Malhotra?"

VIJAY

(voice tight with unease)

"Yes, who is this?"

THE VOICE

"My name is Dr. Pranav. I'm calling from City Specialty Hospital. I'm the duty doctor. Mr. Rishab has been in a serious accident and is currently in the ICU. I urge you to come to the hospital immediately."

VIJAY

(heart pounding, voice shaking with fear)

"Doctor, is he... is he okay? Please, tell me he's okay!"

DR. PRANAV

(calm but urgent)

"Please don't panic. I can't say much right now, but we need you here as soon as possible. Time is critical."

The phone disconnects with a harsh click, leaving Vijay frozen for a moment, the weight of the words sinking in. His breath hitches, and the world suddenly feels unsteady.

SUJATHA

(anxious)

"Who was that? What happened?"

VIJAY

"Rishab's been in an accident. He's in the ICU. Get ready—we need to leave now."

Vijay, Sujatha, and Vivek rush to the City Hospital.

CITY HOSPITAL - 3 AM.

Vijay, along with his wife and son, rush to the ICU on the 3rd floor of the hospital. They meet the duty doctor to inquire about Rishab's condition.

VIJAY

"Doctor, how is Rishab doing now?"

DR. PRANAV

"We'll have to wait until Dr. Madhukar checks on him. He's on his way."

Dr. Madhukar is a senior surgeon and the Medical Director at City Hospital and he also happens to be Vijay's good friend.

Meanwhile, Sujatha stands at the ICU window, her eyes frantically searching for a glimpse of her son. Vijay and Vivek join her, both anxious, hoping to catch sight of Rishab.

Dr. Madhukar arrives swiftly, heading straight to the ICU. He gestures to Vijay and Sujatha as he enters the room. Sujatha is visibly distraught, her tears flowing freely as she struggles to hold herself together. Vijay tries his best to console her, but his words seem powerless.

The family, overwhelmed by fear and uncertainty, spends the night in the hospital lounge, anxiously waiting for news on Rishab's condition.

CITY HOSPITAL – HOSPITAL LOUNGE – 11AM.

Sujatha and Vivek are seated in the hospital lounge. Vivek has dozed off, his head resting on his mother's shoulder. Vijay, restless with worry, paces back and forth in the corridor.

Meanwhile, Dr. Madhukar is performing an emergency surgery on Rishab. The procedure lasts for nearly seven hours.

Rishab's friends and Saira have joined the Malhotras at the hospital, their faces etched with concern.

Finally, after what feels like an eternity, Dr. Madhukar steps out of the surgery room and approaches the lounge.

VIJAY

(anxious)

"Doctor, how is my son? Can we see him now?"

DR. MADHUKAR

"Rishab is out of danger. Come with me."

Sujatha wakes up Vivek and together they begin to
follow Vijay, but Dr. Madhukar stops them.

DR. MADHUKAR

"Please, stay seated in the lounge area for a moment. Saira,
come with me."

Vijay, Saira, and Dr. Madhukar step into the elevator, heading up to the third floor. With each passing floor, Vijay's heartbeat quickens, anxiety building inside him.

They arrive at the entrance to the ICU. Dr. Madhukar opens the door and allows Saira to enter. She approaches Rishab's bed and gently holds his hand. He is unconscious, connected to a ventilator.

Dr. Madhukar and Vijay remain outside the ICU, the door closing softly behind Saira.

DR. MADHUKAR

(speaking to Vijay with calm authority)

"Vijay, please be patient and listen carefully. When Rishab
was brought in, his condition was critical. He had lost a lot
of blood, and his left leg was severely damaged. He had

been lying on the road for nearly two hours and the contaminated water on the road had entered his wounds, causing gangrene to set in. We had no choice but to amputate his left leg to save his life."

The words hit Vijay like a physical blow. His heart seems to stop for a moment, the weight of the news sinking in. He feels the ground beneath him shift, his legs nearly giving way.

VIJAY
(voice trembling, breathless)
"Water... please."

Dr. Madhukar quickly goes to the water purifier in the lobby and fills a glass. He hands it to Vijay, who gulps it down, still feeling unsteady. A cold sweat forms on his brow, and his body begins to tremble with shock.

Dr. Madhukargently guides Vijay to sit down, rubbing his back to calm his anxiety

DR. MADHUKAR
"Breathe, Vijay. It's going to be okay. You need to stay strong now."

Vijay sits there, still struggling to comprehend the magnitude of what has happened, as Dr. Madhukar continues to offer quiet reassurance.

DR. MADHUKAR
"Vijay, let's go to the emergency room."

VIJAY
(in a breathless voice)
"Take me to my son. I want to see him now."

Dr. Madhukar's attempts to calm him are in vain, as Vijay is adamant about seeing Rishab.

CITY HOSPITAL – ICU

Vijay stands frozen at the door, his eyes fixed on his son lying on the bed, connected to an artificial oxygen machine.

The heartbroken father walks slowly but steadily toward Rishab.

He stands beside his son's bed, tears streaming down his face as he gets closer. He gently places a kiss on Rishab's forehead. As his hand trembles, he slowly pulls back the blanket, revealing the amputated leg.

The sight is unbearable for Vijay. Overcome with grief, he collapses into Dr. Madhukar's arms, unable to hold himself together any longer. Saira, who has been standing beside the bed, also catches sight of the amputated leg. Her world shatters in an instant. She stumbles backward, disbelief written across her face, and crashes into the wall.

VIJAY

(grasping for breath, his voice shaking with desperation)

"Doctor, he can't just lie here like this... he needs to get up, he needs to train. The championship trophy is waiting for him."

Dr. Madhukar and the other doctors rush to assist, trying to calm Vijay down. The scene grows chaotic, the weight of the situation bearing down on everyone.

Suddenly, Vijay holds his chest and collapses. He is rushed to the emergency room, but despite the doctors' best efforts with CPR he fails to respond. The doctors work frantically, but ultimately, they are unable to revive Vijay. He dies of a heart attack, his life slipping away just as Rishab fights for his own.

MALHOTRA HOME - DAY

Vijay's body is laid in the Central Hall. Sujatha is sitting beside her husband's lifeless form, silent tears streaming down her cheeks. Saira sits next to her, gently offering comfort.

Vivek stands nearby, accepting condolences from relatives and friends, struggling to keep his emotions in check. The entire staff of MIL arrives to pay their last respects to their beloved boss, the atmosphere heavy with grief and reverence.

CREMATORIUM – EVENING

Vijay's body is laid to rest at the crematorium. The emotions run high as Vivek performs the final rites for his father, his hands trembling with grief, his heart shattering with every ritual. Each gesture feels like a farewell carved in pain, a son's last act of love wrapped in unbearable sorrow.

MALHOTRA HOME - LATE EVENING

An emotionally shattered Sujatha walks into the house, holding Vivek's hand.

She moves slowly to her room and sits on the bed. Looking at Vijay's photograph placed beside her, she bursts into tears, the weight of the loss finally overwhelming her.

In the drawing room, relatives and a few of the employees, including Gupta, who had accompanied Sujatha and Vivek home, wait quietly. Vivek enters the drawing room and with a heavy heart thanks everyone for their support and condolences.

After offering their final words of comfort, the guests leave one by one.

Vivek walks over to Vijay's portrait, adorned with flowers and garlands. Standing before it, he stares at his father's image. The dam of caged emotions finally breaks and he falls to his knees, tears pouring down as he mourns the loss of his beloved father.

Meanwhile, Rishab remains unconscious in the ICU, unaware of the storm that has engulfed both him and his family.

CITY HOSPITAL - DAY

Rishab slowly begins to regain awareness, his senses dull at first, the world around him a blur. As the days pass, he starts to feel the changes in his body, the sharp pangs of pain in his body, a constant reminder of the tragedy that had befallen him.

His eyes flutter open one morning, the sterile white light of the private room greeting him. The gentle hum of medical equipment fills the silence as he takes in his surroundings.

NURSE

(with a warm smile)

"Sir, how are you feeling?"

RISHAB

(in a weak voice)

"Maa?"

The nurse quickly walks to the intercom and dials Dr. Madhukar. The doctor arrives in the ward a few minutes later.

DR. MADHUKAR

(checking the pulse)

"You are doing great young man? Want to see your mother?"

Rishab nods weakly. Dr. Madhukar gestures to the nurse to bring Sujatha to the ward.

CITY HOSPITAL – LOUNGE.

The nurse walks up to Sujatha.

NURSE

"Ma'am, Rishab has regained full consciousness. He's asking for you."

Sujatha's face lights up with hope as she quickly rushes to the ward to see her son.

DR. MADHUKAR

"Sujatha, Rishab has regained full consciousness. We're starting him on a liquid diet today. Feed him some fresh fruit juice. Don't worry, he's recovering well."

SUJATHA

(with a happy tone)

"Thank you, Doctor."

The doctor and the nurse leave the ward. Sujatha moves closer to her son and sits beside him. She places her hand on his forehead and tears of joy flow from her eyes. Rishab smiles faintly at his mother, feeling the warmth of her touch, a tear rolls down his cheek as well. Sujatha quickly wipes it away and kisses him gently on the forehead.

He closes his eyes and falls into a peaceful sleep.

For the next couple of days, Sujatha stays by Rishab's side, nursing him around the clock.

One night, Rishab suddenly experiences an anxiety attack, gasping for air and sweating profusely. The oximeter shows fluctuating readings. His subconscious mind replays the traumatic night of the accident, triggering the attack.

Sujatha, panicked and unsure of what to do, rushes toward the doctor's chamber, shouting for help!!

The duty doctor arrives quickly, attends to Rishab and administers an injection. The medication helps calm him down.

As the days pass, Rishab gradually gains enough strength to sit with his mother's help.

Rishab is woken up by the loud thud of the door. He sees Sujatha entering with a flask in her hand.

SUJATHA

"Good morning, Son."

RISHAB

(smiling weakly, in a low voice)
"Good morning, Maa."

Sujatha approaches the table located on the opposite side of Rishab's bed, looking for a glass to pour the hot coffee from the flask.

RISHAB

"When is Papa coming ?"

Sujatha is taken aback by Rishab's question. Taking a deep breath and gathering all her courage, she turns around to face him.

SUJATHA

"The doctor informed me that you can have solid food from today. What would you like for breakfast?"

Sujatha is trying to avoid her son's question.

RISHAB

"Maa, did Papa come last night? I want to see him."

Sujatha turns to the table once more, tears flowing down her face. She stands still, grappling with the challenge of articulating a reason to her son.

Rishab tries to sit on his own and then the sharp sensation of the loss hits him. He looks down and feels nothing but emptiness where his left leg should be. The revelation devastates him and he cries out in torment, wailing like a soul engulfed in hopelessness....

Sujatha turns around in horror and rushes to her son. She attempts to comfort him, yet Rishab remains beyond consolation. His suffering is boundless.

Hearing Rishab's loud cries, the duty doctor and nurses rush into the ward. The doctor holds Rishab, and tries to calm him down, but he fails as well.

Broken and exhausted Rishab falls unconscious into his mother's arms.

CITY HOSPITAL - EVENING.

Sujatha stands quietly by the window, her eyes lost in the world outside. Children's laughter echoes from the park across the road. She watches them play, a fragile smile tugging at her lips, though her heart is heavy.

Behind her, Rishab lies motionless on the bed, staring blankly at the ceiling. His eyes are hollow, filled with silent suffering. Guilt weighs on him like chains, he blames himself for every tear shed by those he loves, and most of all, for his father's death. The pain gnaws at him constantly.

His body is slowly healing, but his mental health is deteriorating. Each day, he retreats further into silence, shutting out the world — friends, relatives, even the staff who once cared for him with warmth. He doesn't speak. He doesn't respond. He simply exists, haunted and unreachable.

Sujatha watches him fade, helpless and heartbroken. Her once vibrant son is slipping through her fingers, and no amount of love seems enough to hold him back from the darkness.

Dr. Madhukar, seeing the anguish in Sujatha's eyes gently suggests she bring Rishab home. Maybe, the familiar warmth of home can reach the places medicine cannot. He hopes, as does she, that in the comfort of his own walls, Rishab might find his way back to life.

Rishab had finally been discharged from the hospital. The car ride to home was quiet, each passing streetlight casting flickers of memory across his mind. In the front seat, Vivek kept his eyes on the road, stealing glances at his brother through the rearview mirror. Sujatha sat beside Rishab, her presence calm but concerned.

MALHOTRA HOME - LATE EVENING.

Vivek quickly steps out and opens the door for his brother. Rishab reaches for his crutches, hesitating for a moment. His body still ached, but the pain in his chest ran deeper.

Vivek offers his shoulder. Rishab takes it, grateful without words. Slowly, they move together towards the house. Every step up the entrance stairs felt like a mountain, but Rishab pressed on, leaning into his brother's support.

The servants rushed without being called. They didn't speak. They just grabbed the luggage from the car and took it into the house.

As Rishab stepped inside, the familiar scent of home wrapped around him, but he missed something more valuable.

And then he saw his father's portrait hung in the center of the hall. He stared at the photo, as if seeing it for the first time. His breath caught in his throat. He limped forward, slowly, leaning on his crutch as though it were the only thing holding him up.

The closer he got, the more it hurt. When he finally stood in front of the portrait, all the words he hadn't said, all the moments he could never get back, swelled in his chest. His eyes filled with tears.

Behind him, Vivek quietly carried the handbag to Rishab's room. Sujatha came to his side and gently took his arm.

SUJATHA

(Whispering to Rishab)

"Come dear..."

Rishab didn't speak. He just let her guide him, his steps unsteady, the silence between them louder than anything they could have said.

RISHAB'S BEDROOM

He enters the bedroom. Rishab walks slowly to his bed and notices the awards displayed in his personal showcase along the wall.

One award stands out which is placed closest to the bed — the Moto2 Championship Trophy. He reaches out and touches it. In that moment, the weight of everything he's lost crashes over him, and he breaks down in tears.

Sujatha rushes in to console her son.

SUJATHA

(holding back her emotions)

"Son, take some rest."

She gently helps Rishab lie down on the bed. In the days that follow, Rishab remains confined to his bedroom. He refuses to meet anyone who comes to visit. He shuts himself off from the world, retreating into silence and solitude within the four walls.

Meanwhile, Rishab's tragedy has sent shockwaves through Saira's life as well. Overcome with despair, she locks herself in her room. Dr. Rastogi and his wife are deeply worried about their daughter, unsure how to reach her through the sorrow.

RASTOGI HOME - SAIRA'S ROOM

Dr. Rastogi walks into his daughter's room and finds her lying on the sofa, lost in pensive thought. He approaches quietly and sits beside her.

DR. RASTOGI

(in a deep, steady tone)

"How long are you going to stay like this? This state of yours is killing us. I feel bad for Rishab and I am in pain too, but we have to find a way to move forward."

Saira looks at her father with a blank, distant gaze.

DR. RASTOGI

"You are our world, Saira. We can't afford to lose you. I want you to apply for your master's. Please leave this place for a while and give yourself some space. As long as you stay here, these memories will keep haunting you. There's a long road ahead — your career, your ambitions and dreams. Think about it, my child. Your life is in your hands."

He gently kisses her on the forehead and stands to leave. Just then, a notification pops up on Saira's phone, illuminating the screen. Her eyes fall on the background photo — it's from her last ride with Rishab.

Her face crumples. She clutches the phone and begins to weep.

MALHOTRA Home – DAY

Rishab is asleep in his room, while Sujatha tends to her kitchen garden.

Suddenly, the doorbell rings. Hearing it, she wipes her hands and walks toward the front door. She opens it to find Saira standing with her parents. Saira is holding a bouquet of fresh flowers in her hand.

SUJATHA

(with a welcoming smile)

"Please come in."

They all move into the drawing room and settle onto the sofa.

DR. RASTOGI

"Sujatha, how is Rishab doing?"

SUJATHA

(the smile fades and a shadow of pain crosses her face)
"He hasn't left his room since he returned from the
hospital."

Sujatha leads Saira and her parents toward Rishab's room. She quietly opens the door and finds him still fast asleep.

DR. RASTOGI
"Let's not disturb him."

Everyone steps away from the room except Saira. She stays.

She walks slowly to his bedside and looks at him, her eyes full of quiet sorrow. Sitting beside him, a tear slips down her cheek and falls on his hand.

Rishab stirs, blinking awake. He opens his eyes to find Saira sitting next to him. His heart fill with joy. He tries to sit up, struggling against the weakness in his body.

RISHAB
(his voice lit with emotion)
"Saira... I've been waiting for you. Why did you take so long? My heart has been longing to see you."

SAIRA
(softly, almost apologetically)
"I'm sorry... I was caught up with exams."

RISHAB
"It's okay. Don't worry. Will you sit closer to me? You're the only hope I have... the only reason I want to keep going."

He gently takes her hand, but Saira shifts uncomfortably. Her hesitation is clear, her body stiffens and she avoids eye contact.

RISHAB
(drawing her hand to his chest)
"I'll be alright now... with you by my side."

Saira suddenly pulls her hand away. She stands and takes a few steps back.

SAIRA

"Rishab... there's something important I need to tell you. I'm leaving for the UK in a month. I've been accepted into a master's program."

The silence falls like a heavy curtain. Rishab doesn't move. His eyes well up, his breath shallow. The words barely register. Everything inside him seems to collapse.

SAIRA

(gently)

"Please... take care of yourself."

She turns and opens the door, only to find Sujatha standing there, holding a glass of juice. Her expression is pained.

SUJATHA

(deeply hurt)

"I truly hoped you would stay by Rishab's side, help him find his way back to life."

Saira says nothing. With her head low, she walks past Sujatha and quietly leaves with her parents.

MALHOTRA HOME – VIVEK'S ROOM

Rishab enters the room. Vivek gets up from his study table and helps his brother sit on the sofa.

RISHAB

(in a soft tone)

"Vivek, can I ask you for a favour?"

VIVEK

"Bro, please tell me what I can do for you."

RISHAB

"Can you get me a bottle of whiskey? Because nothing else... nothing else can numb the fire tearing through my chest. I've tried to hold on, but this pain...it's unbearable."

Rishab pleads, folding his hands in front of his brother.

Vivek gets up and hugs him tightly. His heart melts seeing the tears in his beloved brother's eyes.

DINING ROOM – LATER THAT NIGHT

Sujatha calls out to Rishab for dinner, but he doesn't respond, concerned she walks to his room and slowly opens the door. Rishab startled tries to hide something. Unaware, Sujatha approaches him.

SUJATHA

"Come, dinner is ready."

RISHAB

(hesitant)

"I'll be there in a minute."

Sujatha senses something is off. She moves closer and catches the smell of alcohol. Leaning slightly, she spots the whiskey bottle under the table. She picks it up and looks at Rishab, who avoids meeting her eyes.

Without a word, an angry Sujatha storms out and goes to Vivek, who is now at the dining table. She holds up the whiskey bottle in front of him. Vivek shivers at the sight. Before he can respond, Sujatha slaps him hard. Her eyes burn with rage. Just then, Rishab enters the dining area.

RISHAB

"Maa, please don't hit Vivek. I asked him to get me the whiskey."

Sujatha remains silent, placing the bottle on the table. She heads to the kitchen, brings out the plates, and sets the table. Rishab sits in front of his plate, lost in thought. Sujatha settles in front of her own plate after serving the food. She looks at Rishab.

SUJATHA

"Rishab, I made your favourite dish today. Please eat."

He doesn't respond and continues staring at his plate. After a few seconds, he looks up at her.

RISHAB
(emotional with tears streaming down his cheeks)
"Maa... I don't want to be a burden on you and Vivek. I've brought this cloud of darkness into our family. I don't deserve to live."

Moved, Sujatha gets up and hugs him tightly.

SUJATHA
(in a pained voice)
"You are the very air I breathe and Vivek is the beat of my heart. If either of you falters, I cease to exist. This is the path God has chosen for us, no matter how cruel it feels. But we will not break — we will stand together and endure this storm, as a family."

Vivek leaps from his chair and embraces his brother.

VIVEK
"Bro... I've always seen you as a winner. Please, don't lose hope."

It's an emotional night for the Malhotra family.

FMSCI office - Conference Room:
The Federation of Motor Sports Clubs of India.

The board members of the FMSCI are meeting to discuss India's representation in the upcoming MotoGP World Championship.

Mr. Behera, the President of the FMSCI, is chairing the meeting.

MR. BEHERA
"Gentlemen, it is unfortunate that Rishab will not be able to represent India in the next year's British MotoGP. The next contender in line is Vinod, who is eligible to compete

in the championship. We must inform the JMC Racing Team about this development so that they can formally withdraw from the tournament."

All the board members agree with Mr. Behera and unanimously approve Vinod's participation in the British MotoGP Championship.

The FMSCI authorities begin processing the required approvals. The necessary paperwork and formalities are being prepared and sent to the FIM - Fédération Internationale de Motocyclisme, the world governing body for motorcycle racing.

Vinod receives a phone call from the FMSCI office. Srinivasan, the Secretary of the FMSCI informs him of his selection to compete in the British Motogp championship.

Hearing the news, Vinod jumps up in ecstasy. An explosion of joy. A cry of triumph escaping his lips. He rushes to his family, shouting the news. Hugs and laughter fill the room. His happiness knew no bounds.

Back at Malhotra Industries, things have begun to fall apart in the absence of the leadership.

The demise of Vijay Malhotra and Rishab's continued absence from work has jeopardized several key projects, including the ambitious JMC project.

The board members and company directors are under immense pressure to meet project delivery deadlines. The delays in completing the JMC project have raised serious concerns among the Japanese management.

The JMC executives are increasingly dissatisfied with the situation at Malhotra Industries and are now growing anxious about their investments in the project.

MALHOTRA HOME – DRAWING ROOM

Two senior directors of Malhotra Industries, Virender Singh and Mallikarjun Patil arrive to visit Rishab and

Sujatha at their home. As usual, Rishab refuses to meet them.

The directors sit with Sujatha, trying to explain the seriousness of the situation at the office.

VIRENDER SINGH

"Ma'am, our contract with JMC is in jeopardy. We're struggling to get the infrastructure ready to kick-start the manufacturing process. The development team is waiting on Rishab. We need him back in the office as soon as possible."

SUJATHA

"Mr. Singh, you've seen Rishab's condition. I'm not sure he'll be able to return to the office anytime soon."

MALLIKARJUN

(a veteran in the company)

"Sujatha, I don't think you understand the gravity of the situation. If this continues, we risk losing major projects and slipping into a financial crisis. Our partners, especially JMC is starting to lose faith in us. I understand what you're going through, but without strong leadership at MIL, we can't move forward."

MALLIKARJUN

(continues after a pause)

"I think it's time we consider taking Rishab to a psychiatrist."

Sujatha bursts into tears upon hearing Mallikarjun's suggestion. The men try to console her. After composing herself, she speaks to both directors.

SUJATHA

"Please... just give me some more time. I believe everything will be all right soon."

Reassured by her words, the directors take their leave. Though Sujatha has given them hope, deep inside, she is unsure — both about Rishab and the future of the company.

She walks over to Vijay's portrait and breaks down, weeping helplessly, uncertain of the path ahead.

Just then, there's a knock at the door. Sujatha wipes her tears, turns around, and walks to the entrance. Standing at the doorstep is a young woman with a warm smile. Sujatha is struck by the radiance on her face and the sparkle in her eyes.

CHETHANA
(smiling)
"Namaste..."

Sujatha returns the smile and welcomes her inside.

SUJATHA
(with a hint of doubt)
"Sorry, I think I've seen you somewhere before."

CHETHANA
(smiling)
"Yes, ma'am. We've met before. My name is Chethana and I'm the manager at Karunya, which is run by your family trust."

SUJATHA
(recollecting)
"Oh..yes, Chethana.... Vijay had introduced you during a celebration at the old age home.
Come, dear. Please sit. I'll get you some coffee."

CHETHANA
"Sure, ma'am."

Sujatha heads to the kitchen to prepare coffee. Meanwhile, Chethana strolls through the drawing room, taking in the surroundings. Her eyes settle on a showcase filled with medals and trophies. As she walks past, she stops in front of Vijay Malhotra's portrait and stands still, gazing at it. Her eyes fill with tears.

Just then, Sujatha returns with a cup of coffee in her hand.

SUJATHA

"Come dear, please have a seat."

She hands the cup to Chethana, and they both sit on the sofa in the central hall.

CHETHANA

(hesitantly)

"Ma'am, I have something important to share."

SUJATHA

"Of course,. Go ahead."

CHETHANA

"Ma'am, we're facing a problem at Karunya. Since Vijay sir's passing, the funds have stopped coming in and it's been three months now. The old age home is struggling to meet even the daily needs. Karunya needs your help."

Karunya, an Old Age Home which houses around 60 residents is operated by the Malhotra Family Trust.

Sujatha is shocked. She's deeply hurt, knowing how much Vijay cared for the residents, treating them like his own family and always ensuring they had the best care.

Without hesitation, she goes to her room and returns with some cash. She hands the money to Chethana.

SUJATHA

"Chethana, please take this and use it to meet the immediate needs. I'll make sure the monthly funds are resumed and credited to Karunya's account without any further delay. I sincerely apologize for what happened."

Chethana gratefully accepts the money.

CHETHANA

"Thank you so much, ma'am. Please do visit Karunya sometime."

SUJATHA

"Of course, dear. I'll visit soon."

After bidding goodbye to Chethana, Sujatha quietly walks toward Rishab's room.

RISHAB'S ROOM

Sujatha sees Rishab lying on the bed, staring blankly out of the window.

SUJATHA

(in a low, firm voice)

"So... how long do you plan to lock yourself in this room? Rishab, we're running out of time. This isn't just about you anymore, it's about the thousand employees working at our company. Their future and the future of their families is at stake if we don't start controlling the damage that's happening."

SUJATHA

(continues after a pause)

"Your father built an old age home to care for people who are abandoned and left on the streets. Today, even they are struggling to meet their basic needs. You must step out of these four walls for the people who are depending on us. I'm sorry if my words hurt you. But as your mother, I have to remind you of your responsibilities."

SUJATHA

(soft tone)

"Unfortunately, I'm not educated enough to handle the company's affairs... and Vivek is still studying."

Sujatha turns and walks out of the room.

Rishab lies motionless, clearly disturbed by his mother's words. He feels overwhelmed, still believing he's not mentally or physically ready to face the world. But her words linger in his mind.

He picks up his phone and scrolls through his contacts. Desperate, he decides to call his close friends, hoping they can help pull him out of his depression. He dials Nikhil.

NIKHIL'S HOME – Same Time

NIKHIL

(answering)

"Hey Rishab! How are you, mate?"

RISHAB

"Buddy... it's been a while. Can we meet today? I haven't stepped out of the house in days. Can you take me to our regular coffee spot this evening?"

NIKHIL

"I'd love to, Rishab... but I'm flying to New York tonight for a project. I'm so sorry, buddy."

RISHAB

"No worries. I understand. Have a safe trip."

NIKHIL

"Thanks, man. Oh—and I forgot to tell you, Sid got married last week."

RISHAB

(surprised)

"What? That's a shock. He didn't even tell me."

NIKHIL

"Yeah... he's in Goa right now, on his honeymoon."

RISHAB

"I'll call and congratulate him."

Rishab ends the call. He feels a pang of sadness, hurt that his best friend didn't inform him about something so important. Still, he decides to call Sid.

GOA – BEACH RESORT – SUNSET

Sid is at a beachside counter, waiting for a drink. Natasha, his wife, picks up a ringing phone.

NATASHA

(calling out)
"Sid... it's Rishab."

Sid walks over. He looks at the screen, hesitates... and then silently declines the call, slipping the phone into his pocket.

SID

"Just a friend. I'll call him once we're back."

RISHAB'S ROOM

Rishab stares at the screen, realizing Sid cut the call, disappointed but not ready to give up, he dials Ashish next.

No answer.... The phone is switched off. Frustrated, angry and heartbroken, Rishab throws his phone against the floor. It smashes into pieces.

MALHOTRA HOME – TERRACE – LATE EVENING

Rishab stands alone on the terrace, gazing up at the star-lit sky. The night is calm, the silence comforting. Sujatha walks in quietly and stands beside her son. They exchange a warm smile, then continue looking at the sky together.

RISHAB

"Maa."

Sujatha turns to face him, sensing something in his voice.

RISHAB

(with a firm tone)
"I've decided to return to the office."

Relief washes over Sujatha. Without saying a word, she embraces him tightly, her eyes welling with emotion.

Though the days ahead will be challenging, Rishab has taken the first step, accepting his new reality will take time.

Rishab accompanied by his mother and brother visit the hospital — beginning his journey toward healing, acceptance, and responsibility.

CITY SPECIALITY HOSPITAL – DR. MADHUKAR'S CABIN

The experts enter the room carrying the specially designed wooden limb for Rishab. Dr. Madhukar, along with his team, carefully fits the wooden leg onto Rishab's stump. The doctors then gently help him to his feet.

Rishab takes his initial steps cautiously, holding onto his mother for support. With each step, his confidence grows. Soon, he begins to walk independently — limping slightly, but determined. His eyes fill with joy as he moves around the cabin, testing his new leg.

Sujatha watches with tear-filled eyes, overwhelmed with emotion as she sees her son take his first steps toward a new beginning.

DR. MADHUKAR

"Well done my boy!! Your father always believed in you. He wanted you to be a champion and he held on to that dream until his very last breath. I have no doubt he would be proud of the steps you took today."

RISHAB

(anxiously)

"Doctor... what were my father's last words?"

DR. MADHUKAR

"He said... he wanted to see you become a world champion."

Rishab breaks down in tears, overwhelmed by the weight of his father's final wish. Rishab begins practicing walking with the artificial wooden leg over the course of a week. However, he struggles with certain tasks — climbing stairs, wearing his trousers and occasionally injuring his stump by putting too much pressure on his left leg.

One day he takes a bad fall while attempting to go down the stairs, but fortunately escapes unhurt as Vivek rushes just in time to hold him.

Rishab decides to use crutches for additional support while walking with the wooden leg.

MALHOTRA HOME – EVENING

Sujatha greets Gupta who is visiting the family that evening. He meets only Sujatha and spends some time discussing something important.

RISHAB'S ROOM – MORNING, 8:00 AM

Rishab is getting ready to go to the office. He sits down and adjusts his wooden limb. He puts on his casual clothes and stands in front of the mirror.

Rishab has gained weight — his stomach is protruding and a thick beard covers his face. A pained smile appears as he looks at himself in the mirror.

MALHOTRA INDUSTRIES

Rishab walks into the building with the help of crutches.

As he enters the reception area, he sees the staff waiting for him. They rejoice and welcome him warmly. The receptionist approaches and applies a holy teeka on his forehead. One of the directors present him with a bouquet. The rest of the staff comes forward to greet him.

Rishab thanks them and begins walking toward his cabin on the first floor.

LIFT LOBBY

As Rishab reaches the lift lobby, he sees Gupta. The two men exchange a brief, emotional smile.

GUPTA

(with a pained tone)

"Good morning, sir. How are you?"

RISHAB

(with a strained tone)
"Good morning, Guptaji. I'm doing well... I'm alive.I shouted at you that day and didn't care about your injury. Look at me now....standing in front of you without a leg."

His voice is filled with pain and remorse. Rishab folds his hands in front of Gupta.

RISHAB (CONT'D)

"Please accept my apologies. I'm ashamed of my behavior."

Gupta steps forward and embraces Rishab in a tight, heartfelt hug.

GUPTA

"You are my Vijay's son. I can only offer you blessings."

It was indeed an emotional meet.

@ MIL - PMO OFFICE

As Rishab walks past the Project Management Office, something catches his attention. He steps inside and notices the KANBAN board hanging on the wall. It displays the current status of projects at MIL. The majority of projects are marked in red and behind schedule.

He quietly exits the PMO and continues walking toward his cabin. On the way, he stops at his father's cabin. As he enters, he feels a strong sense of Vijay's presence. Rishab spends the rest of the day sitting alone in the cabin, unsure of what to do or where to begin.

MONTAGE – A WEEK PASSES

Rishab is yet to take charge of the company's affairs. He wanders through the office aimlessly, barely acknowledging greetings from the staff. His distant, distracted behaviour during meetings becomes a growing concern for the management.

MIL – RISHAB'S CABIN – MORNING

Mallikarjun walks into Rishab's cabin.

MALLIKARJUN

"Rishab, JMC management has confirmed on the meeting for 2 PM today. I hope the project plan is ready? We need to win back their confidence."

RISHAB

"Yes, Mr. Mallik. We're good."

Mallikarjun, visibly relieved, nods and exits the cabin.

MIL – CONFERENCE ROOM – 2:00 PM

Mallikarjun and the senior executives sit in the conference room, waiting for Rishab. But he doesn't show up. A worried Mallikarjun calls Rishab's phone — it's switched off. He rushes to Rishab's cabin on the first floor, only to find it empty.

METRO RACE TRACK – NIGHT

Security personnel are on patrol near the race track. One of the guards notices something unusual on the track, but the darkness makes it hard to clearly identify the object.

1ST SECURITY GUARD

"Hey, look, there's something weird on the track."

2ND SECURITY GUARD

"Let me check."

The second guard cautiously approaches the object, keeping a safe distance. He flashes his torchlight and to his surprise, finds Rishab lying on the track. As the beam hits Rishab's face, he flinches and covers his eyes, the light is too harsh.

2ND SECURITY GUARD

(concerned)

"Sorry sir, Are you okay?"

Both guards help Rishab to his feet.

1ST SECURITY GUARD

"Sir, should we drop you at the parking area?"

RISHAB

"No, I'm good. Thanks."

As Rishab limps away from the track, the two guards silently watch him disappear into the darkness.

MALHOTRA HOME – MIDNIGHT

Rishab enters the house and walks into the drawing room. He finds Sujatha asleep on the sofa, having dozed off while waiting for him.

As he heads toward the bedroom, he accidentally knocks over a flower vase perched on the edge of the wall. It crashes to the floor with a loud shatter, startling Sujatha awake.

She quickly rushes toward Rishab.

SUJATHA

(anxiously)

"Where have you been? I called you a dozen times! People from the office tried reaching you too!"

Rishab doesn't respond. He silently walks into his bedroom.

RISHAB'S ROOM – BATHROOM

Rishab steps into the bathroom and stares at his reflection in the mirror. His face is weary, eyes bloodshot, his beard unkempt — a man visibly carrying the weight of grief and guilt. He turns on the tap and splashes cold water on his face, hoping to shake off the numbness.

But as the water drips down, something inside him breaks. He grips the edges of the sink, his breathing quickens, his eyes well up and then he suddenly breaks down, sobbing uncontrollably.

His reflection blurs through the tears, but he keeps staring, almost as if searching for the man he once was.

MALHOTRA'S HOME - AT THE DINING TABLE

Chethana is visiting Sujatha for lunch.

CHETHANA

"Ma'am, you have magical fingers. Every dish on the table
is delicious. The bhindi reminds me of my mother's
cooking."

Chethana had lost her mother a couple of years ago, and
Sujatha was well aware of it.

SUJATHA

"Dear, how do you manage the kitchen with both of you
working ?"

CHETHANA

(smiling)

"We wake up early. Baba helps me in the kitchen."

SUJATHA

(with a pained tone)

"Dear, you know what Rishab is going through. He's
completely lost. I feel like he's burning out, bit by bit,
every single day."

A pause. A quiet heaviness settles in the room.

SUJATHA

"I don't know why... but I feel you can bring him back to
life. I need your help."

Another pause. Her voice cracks.

SUJATHA

(folding her hands, tears rolling down)

"Please... save my son."

Chethana quickly rises from her chair and embraces
Sujatha tightly.

CHETHANA

"Ma'am... please don't do this."

SUJATHA

"Can you... call me Maa?"

Chethana's eyes fill with tears.

CHETHANA
"Maa, I'll try my best..."

CHAPTER THREE

THE JOURNEY

MIL OFFICE – RISHAB'S CABIN – DAY

Rishab stands near the window, a cigarette in hand. A soft knock on the door breaks his thoughts.

SECRETARY

"Sir, Chethana from Karunya Trust is here to see you."

The secretary hands him a visiting card.

RISHAB

"Please ask her to come in."

He quickly stubs out the cigarette and walks over to his chair.

A moment later, there's another knock. A young woman stands at the door, smiling warmly. As Chethana enters, she subtly reacts to the lingering smell of smoke. Rishab notices and is visibly embarrassed.

CHETHANA

"Good morning, Mr. Rishab."

RISHAB

"Good morning, Chethana. Please, have a seat."

As she settles in, Rishab continues.

RISHAB

"Apologies for the smell and the mess — things have been a little chaotic around here. I'm working on fixing it. I've asked the finance team to ensure the monthly funds are

transferred to the Trust without delay."
CHETHANA
(with gratitude)
"Thank you so much, Mr. Rishab. I'd also like to invite you to visit Karunya. The inmates are very eager to meet you."
She pauses, then speaks more softly.
CHETHANA
(in a low tone)
"Vijay Sir treated the residents at Karunya as his own. He always made time to visit them every week.
I hope you'll continue what he started... and be there for them."
Rishab, moved struggles to find the right words.
RISHAB
(softly, voice slightly strained)
"I'll... probably visit them this weekend."
CHETHANA
"Great! How about Sunday? I'll be at your place at 9 AM sharp to pick you up."
Rishab looks surprised by her direct offer, but before he can respond, Chethana rises from her chair, smiles and quietly exits the room.

MALHOTRA'S HOME – SUNDAY MORNING
Rishab wakes up early that morning and gets ready to visit the oldage home.
Chethana arrives at the gate on her scooter. She spots Sujatha on the terrace, watering the plants. Chethana honks and Sujatha looks down. They wave to each other.
SUJATHA
"Please come in dear.."

CHETHANA

"Maa it's getting late. Could you please check if Rishab is ready? We need to be at Karunya before breakfast time."

Sujatha is slightly surprised, Rishab hadn't mentioned this visit to her. She quickly heads inside to check on him.

RISHAB'S BEDROOM

As Sujatha enters, she finds Rishab putting on his shoes. She quickly rush and kneels down to help him.

SUJATHA

(in a cheerful tone)

"Rishab, Chethana is here. She's waiting for you at the gate."

RISHAB

(with a hint of guilt)

"Sorry, Maa. I forgot to tell you about today's visit to Karunya. Chethana asked me to come and I thought I'd meet everyone there... see how things are going."

SUJATHA

"Sure, son."

Rishab gets up, takes his crutches and heads toward the door. Sujatha stops him and opens the cupboard. She pulls out a blue jacket and helps him wear it.

SUJATHA

"My son is looking handsome today."

Rishab smiles and thanks her with a warm hug and then heads to the main gate.

AT THE GATE

Rishab and Chethana greet each other warmly. Rishab looks at the scooter with mild hesitation.

RISHAB

"Let me ask the driver to bring the car. You can park your scooter here."

CHETHANA

"I love riding my scooter. Come, I'll help you get on."

Rishab surrenders to her enthusiasm and agrees with a smile.

CHETHANA

"Okay — let's go!"

Rishab smiles again and gently holds her shoulder for support as he gets on.

ON THE ROAD

As they ride, Rishab experiences a surprising sense of joy. He closes his eyes for a moment, letting the cool breeze hit his face.

This is his first ride on a two-wheeler since the accident and he savours every second of it.

KARUNYA – ENTRANCE

They arrive at the gates of the old age home.

Karunya is a two-story building with a beautifully manicured lawn in the front. The structure is enclosed by high walls and a large gate. The watchman quickly opens the gate, allowing Chethana's scooter to enter. She parks in front of the reception area and Rishab slowly gets down. It's his first visit to the old age home. He takes a moment to look around, observing the peaceful surroundings as he walks toward the reception area with Chethana.

CHETHANA

(in an excited tone)

"Welcome to Karunya."

Rishab finds the place calm and peaceful. He and Chethana walk toward the central hall. There he notices a portrait of Vijay Malhotra. He steps closer and gazes at it, lost in thought. From behind, Chethana gently calls out to him.

Rishab turns and to his surprise, sees a dozen elderly residents standing in a line, smiling warmly. Behind them stands Chethana, watching quietly.

One of the residents, an elderly woman in her early 80s, walks forward and offers Rishab a small bouquet of flowers. He accepts it with a soft, appreciative smile.

CHETHANA

"This is Rishab our Vijay-ji's son. He will be your caretaker from now on."

Hearing this, the residents step forward and begin to bless Rishab, some place their hands gently on his head, others kiss his hand with affection. Rishab is deeply moved by their gesture. His eyes fill with tears.

Just then, an elderly gentleman emerges from behind, dressed in a formal suit he approaches Rishab and extends his hand in welcome.

THE OLD MAN
(smiling)

"I'm retired Captain Chatterjee. Sorry for being late. I started early from home but got caught in traffic."

Rishab shakes hands with Mr. Chatterjee.

CHETHANA

"This is our beloved Captain uncle. He's deeply involved in social service and spends most of his time here at Karunya, supporting both the inmates and the staff."

Cpt.CHATTERJEE

"I served my country in the army and after retirement, I chose to serve the people. It brings me joy to help the residents here at Karunya."

Rishab smiles and thanks Cpt. Chatterjee for his dedication.

Chethana begins introducing Rishab to the inmates.

CHETHANA

"There are a few more inmates in their rooms. They couldn't come out due to their physical conditions — some are very old, and a few are paralyzed."

After a pause...

CHETANA
(continues)

"Okay, it's breakfast time. Let's head to the dining area. The inmates are excited to have breakfast with you."

RISHAB

"Sure. I'm happy to dine with them too..!!"

As everyone walks toward the dining area, Rishab turns to Chethana.

RISHAB

"Chethana, how many inmates live here ?"

CHETHANA

"We have 60 people in total."

RISHAB

"Do we have enough rooms to accommodate everyone?"

CHETHANA

"We have 15 rooms and 3 large dormitories. The bedridden inmates are given rooms, while the rest sleep in the dormitories."

They enter the dining area.

DINING AREA

The dining room is spacious with neatly arranged tables and chairs where the residents enjoy their daily meals. Some of the inmates begin laying plates on the tables as the cooks arrive, carrying large vessels. This morning's breakfast is poha — cooked with onions, potatoes, curry leaves, and a dash of lemon. The delicious aroma fills the air.

Rishab looks around, smiling as he observes the joy on the faces of the inmates, all thoroughly enjoying their meal. He takes a bite of the poha and enjoys it too.

Chethana moves from table to table, filling cups with hot coffee. She wears a warm, beautiful smile as she serves. She reaches Rishab's table, places a glass in front of him and pours steaming coffee from the kettle.

RISHAB

"Chethana, please join us for breakfast"

CHETHANA

"Not now. I'll have it later. Need to serve breakfast to the inmates in their rooms. Unfortunately, two of our caretakers left last month."

RISHAB

"Why did they leave?"

CHETHANA

"Their salaries were pending."

Rishab lowers his eyes, feeling a wave of guilt.

CHETHANA

(gently, changing the subject)

"How's the poha ?"

RISHAB

"Yes, it tastes really good."

Just then, a dog enters the dining area. It's brown in color with a collar around its neck. As soon as he sees the dog, Cpt. Chatterjee rises from his chair and calls out.

Cpt. CHATTERJEE

"Rocket! Come here... You didn't get your friend for breakfast today?"

Rocket looks around briefly, then turns and runs out of the dining hall. The dog runs toward the staircase and climbs to the first floor of the building.

ROOM NO. 13 – FIRST FLOOR

An elderly man sits on his bed, wearing dark glasses. He appears to be waiting for someone. Hearing Rocket's whine, the man gets up and reaches for a chain resting on the shelf beside his bed.

OLD MAN
(smiling)

"Good morning Rocket..."

Rocket comes and sits near the old man's feet. The man attaches the chain to Rocket's collar. Once the chain is secured, Rocket gently starts walking out of the room, guiding the old man, who is blind. The old man grips the chain tightly and follows Rocket down the hallway.

DINING ROOM – CONTINUOUS

Rocket leads the old man into the dining hall and gently guides him to his chair. The man lovingly runs his hand over Rocket's back, then unclips the chain. Rocket immediately trots off to his usual spot and begins eating his poha.

Rishab, watching this unfold, is struck with emotion — speechless. Cpt. Chatterjee glances at him with a knowing smile.

Cpt. CHATTERJEE

"Sometimes I feel animals have more humanity than humans..."

After breakfast, Rishab expresses a desire to visit the inmates who couldn't come to the dining hall. Chatterjee agrees and accompanies him.

Rishab walks through the old age home, visiting various rooms. Many of the residents are too old to get out of bed. Some are paralyzed and completely bedridden.

The sight is heartbreaking for him. Rishab enters one of the rooms and finds an old man lying on the bed, while a woman gently massaging his legs.

Cpt. CHATTERJEE

"This is Ramdas and that's his wife, Lakshmi. They've been here for almost two years now.
A road accident four years ago left him paralyzed from the waist down."

RISHAB

"What about their children?"

Cpt. CHATTERJEE

(with a pained smile)

"Like many here, Ramdas has children — two sons and a daughter, but sadly they're all too busy to care for their bedridden father and mother. No one seems to have time for the elderly anymore..."

He pauses, then gestures across the hall to the opposite room.

Cpt. CHATTERJEE

"See the man in that room? We don't even know his real name. We call him Raju. He was rescued from the streets by an NGO. When he arrived, he was in a terrible state — unkempt, disoriented. It took us a while to clean him up and settle him in. Everyone here has a story, Rishab. Your father, Vijay wanted them to live their remaining days in dignity and with a little happiness."

Rishab's eyes fill with tears. He walks down the stairs slowly along with Captain Chatterjee and heads toward the main hall. There, he notices several framed paintings hanging on the wall.

RISHAB

"Sir, who made these?"

Cpt. CHATTERJEE

(in an excited tone)

"These were painted by Ramdas. Chethana had them framed and hung here."

Rishab studies each painting carefully. There's a rose, an old man with a dog, and a portrait of a beautiful woman.

RISHAB

(Pointing at the paintings)

"I think I recognize each of these."

Cpt. CHATTERJEE

"Are you sure ?"

RISHAB

"This is the flower from the garden... and that's Rocket with his dear friend."

Cpt. CHATTERJEE

(smiling)

"You're brilliant."

Rishab moves closer to the last painting. He gently runs his fingers along the frame — he knows the woman in the portrait is Chethana.

RISHAB

(softly)

"Ramdas has magical fingers."

Rishab and Captain Chatterjee walk into the garden. They sit on a bench placed in a quiet corner.

The garden is in full bloom, filled with vibrant flowers and lush green grass that stretches out like a soft carpet. The scene is peaceful and mesmerizing for Rishab.

RISHAB

"Sir, where do you live?"

Cpt. CHATTERJEE

"I stay in Anand Nagar. But I come here every day and leave only around 8 PM. I served in the Indian army for 35 years. I have a son and a daughter — both of them are settled in the US with their families. Unfortunately, I lost my beautiful wife a couple of years ago.."

After a pause....

Cpt. CHATTERJEE
(continues)

"My children are so busy with their lives that they hardly find time to visit me. They keep asking me to move to the US and settle with them."

He pauses again, then smiles faintly.

Cpt. CHATTERJEE

"I spent many years risking my life to protect the borders of the country but now my own children want me to leave this place. But I've decided — I'm not going anywhere. I will take my last breath here."

RISHAB

(in a guilty tone)

"I'm sorry, sir. I know the inmates went through a tough time over the past couple of months. Things really got out of control."

Cpt. CHATTERJEE

"Yes, Karunya struggled after Vijay's passing. But then, the Hunger Warriors came in like messiahs and helped these orphans when we needed it most."

RISHAB

(curious)

"Hunger Warriors ?"

Cpt. CHATTERJEE

"Yes, two young men. When Karunya was struggling to provide three meals a day, they stepped in and ensured we had dinner every night for three months. Some days we had plenty of food, some days just enough. But no one ever complained. Everyone shared what we had and found joy in it."

Just then, Chethana walks into the garden to join Chatterjee and Rishab.

Rishab

"I want to meet the Hunger Warriors. Chethana, is it possible to meet them today?"

Chethana

"Sure, we can meet them. Give me 15 minutes, I need to check if everything is taken care of in the kitchen for lunch and dinner."

Chethana steps out of the kitchen after ensuring everything is in place for the day.

After bidding goodbye to Chatterjee and the inmates, Rishab and Chethana hop onto the scooter and zoom off toward the Hunger Warriors' office, which is a 15-minute ride from the orphanage.

A BUILDING COMPLEX – AFTERNOON

Chethana and Rishab arrive at the Hunger Warriors' office located on the 3rd floor of the building. They take the elevator and walk a few steps from the lobby to an apartment door.

Chethana knocks. After a few seconds, a young man opens the door and smiles warmly upon seeing her. The young man, Madan, welcomes them.

Chethana

"Hello Madan."

Madan

"Welcome Chethana. Please come in."

Chethana turns to her right to introduce Rishab. Madan and Rishab shake hands. The office is a modest one-bedroom apartment. Rishab looks around and notices a man speaking on the phone, jotting down details on a sheet of paper.

Madan

"We just got a call from a party organizer. There's some left over food from a birthday celebration."

Chethana

"Oh, that's great."

Shyam

(holding a sheet of paper)

"Hi Chethana. Who's this with you?"

Chethana

"This is Rishab. His family runs Karunya."

Both Madan and Shyam are happy to meet Rishab.

Rishab

(with a tone of guilt)

"I really want to thank you both for everything you did for the people at Karunya."

Madan

"No worries, mate. Glad we could help."

Rishab

"Is this an NGO ?"

Shyam

"It's neither an NGO, nor do we see it as social service,we understand hunger because we've lived through it."

Rishab

"Whatever you're doing is truly noble. How do you manage to feed so many people?"

Madan

"We've shared our contact details with hotels, community halls, and a few housing societies. Whenever there's surplus food, they call us. We collect it and distribute it across orphanages, old age homes, and shelters. We also go out looking for those in need. It's not hard to spot someone with an empty stomach."

Rishab

"And what about you guys? What do you do for a living?"

Shyam

"We used to work in a big corporate as software engineers. We quit a year ago to fight hunger full-time. Now we do freelance coding — it pays just enough to get by."

Rishab

(in a surprised tone)

"You left high-paying jobs to feed people. What inspired that decision?"

SHYAM

(in a pained tone)

"I still remember that night."

CUT TO FLASHBACK:

SHYAM AND MADAN'S BUILDING – MIDNIGHT – AT THE GATE.

Shyam and Madan return late from an office party. They get out of a cab, Madan walks toward the gate while Shyam stays back to settle the fare.

Madan hears commotion near a garbage bin beside the building compound, curious, he walks along the wall and peeks over. To his horror, he sees a man in torn clothes with long hair and a scraggly beard, fighting with stray dogs over discarded food. In the scuffle, the man is bitten, but he pushes through, desperate to gather more from the bin.

The sight shocks Madan. Without thinking, he runs to intervene. Shyam, now done with the cab, notices the chaos and rushes over. He sees Madan chasing the dogs away with a stick he picked up from the street.

Shyam joins in and together they manage to scare the dogs off.

They turn their attention to the man who is bleeding, but unfazed. He hurriedly stuffs the leftover food into a plastic bag and begins to run.

MADAN

"Wait! Are you okay?"

The man doesn't respond. He just keeps moving. Madan and Shyam follow. Though he's quick, they manage to keep pace. After a 10-minute chase they see the man enter one of the shanty in an open field. Moments later, he emerges carrying a small box. He gently opens it, revealing a tiny kitten inside.

The man places the food on the ground and begins feeding the kitten.

Shyam and Madan stand still in the moonlight, watching the man and his companion eat in silence.

CUT TO PRESENT:

SHYAM

"A man who fought the dogs to feed his little cat.!! The next morning, we returned to that spot but he was gone. No one living in the area knew anything about him. What we saw there changed us. The people living in in-human conditions. The place was unhygienic and overcrowded.

They shared stories of hunger. The daily wages were barely enough to survive, children and the elderly were deprived of nutritious food. It broke our hearts. That's when we decided we had to do something. During our research, we discovered that over a million people die of hunger every year in our country."

Hearing Shyam, Rishab takes a deep breath.

Something on the wall catches his attention. He walks over and reads the quote stuck on the wall:

"The hunger for love is much more difficult to remove than the hunger for bread"

SHYAM

"Sorry, we have to rush to the community hall. Need to

pick up some food."
RISHAB
"Can we come along?"

Madan, Shyam and Chethana exchange surprised glances but they're clearly delighted by Rishab's offer.

COMMUNITY HALL

The Hunger Warriors along with Chethana and Rishab arrive at the destination.

The community hall in-charge greets them and leads the group to the kitchen. He hands over three large covers and containers filled with leftover food.

RISHAB
(whispering to Chethana)
"So much food left over from the party... Unbelievable!!"

After thanking the in-charge, the Hunger Warriors put the covers into their rubber bags and carry the containers by hand. Rishab watches as the young men carefully balance the food bags and containers on their motorcycle, clearly struggling.

CITY STREET – MOMENTS LATER

They ride through the streets. Soon, they spot a group of people sitting on the sidewalk. Madan pulls the bike closer to the pavement and stops. Chethana follows behind. Shyam and Madan open the bags and begin distributing food packets to the people on the pavement. Suddenly, young children from a nearby slum come running the moment they spot the Hunger Warriors.

Shyam hands a few packets to Rishab and Chethana.

SHYAM
"Here, pass these to the kids."

The children stand in front of Rishab, their eyes fixed on the food packets. Rishab gently hands them the food. Their faces light up with joy the moment they receive it.

A woman carrying a toddler calls out emotionally:

WOMAN

"Tonight, my kids won't cry... they have food to eat. Thank you!"

Rishab feels the powerful joy of giving.

MADAN

"These families are daily wage workers from the nearby factory which is now locked down. It is tough times for them."

CITY JUNCTION – LATER

After feeding the slum dwellers, the Hunger Warriors, Chethana and Rishab continue their journey.

At a junction, they find an old man sleeping on the pavement. The team approaches. The man appears weak and frail, unable to sit up. Shyam quickly pulls out a water bottle from his bag and gently cleans the old man's hands and face. They speak to him and learn that he's homeless and it's been days since he last ate.

Rishab's eyes well up with tears. The old man takes the food and eats with pure joy.

MONTAGE – AROUND THE CITY

The team visits underpasses, alleyways and open grounds. They serve food to homeless people, mentally ill destitute and anyone with an empty stomach. Each packet is handed over with care and compassion.

HW OFFICE – EVENING

The Hunger Warriors thank Rishab and Chethana for accompanying them.

MADAN

"Thank you both for joining us today."

RISHAB

"Thank you for showing me the reality of the world we live in. It's heartbreaking to see so many people still struggling for a single meal... so many left uncared for."

MADAN

"Our dream is to build a community kitchen, a place where we can serve even more people who are struggling for their meal."

Rishab steps forward and embraces both Madan and Shyam warmly.

COFFEE SHOP – LATER THAT EVENING

Rishab and Chethana sit at a corner table, sipping coffee. The evening traffic hums in the background.

RISHAB

"I'm truly moved by those two men. When most people are caught in the rat race for money and fame, Shyam and Madan are out there doing selfless work fighting hunger in their own way."

Chethana smiles. She gently holds Rishab's hand, proud and hopeful.

Rishab rides back home with Chethana, a smile on his face. For the first time, he begins to experience true happiness.

MALHOTRA HOME – MAIN GATE

Chethana drops Rishab at his home. He gets off the scooter, still wearing a smile.

RISHAB

"Thank you for making my day."

They exchange a warm goodbye. Chethana rides off into the night while Rishab stands at the gate for a moment, watching her leave, a content smile on his face.

He turns to walk inside, feeling a sense of fulfilment he's

never known before.

BALCONY

Rishab opens the door and steps onto the balcony. The moon shines brightly, and the stars decorate the night sky. He takes a deep breath, enjoying the cool air filling his lungs and admires the beautiful flowers in the balcony.

Just then, Sujatha enters the balcony.

SUJATHA

"Rishab, how are things at Karunya?"

Rishab turns to his mother, smiling.

RISHAB

"Maa, your garden is beautiful. No wonder you spend so much time here."

Sujatha is both surprised and overjoyed at her son's words.

SUJATHA

"Thank you, son."

RISHAB

"Maa, we need to do so much more for the inmates at Karunya. I'll make sure they live a happy and dignified life in our old age home."

Sujatha gives her son a warm hug, feeling a deep sense of pride. She knows that the day's experience has had a positive impact on Rishab's heart and mind.

DINING ROOM

It's a special dinner. Rishab savours his mother's biryani and halwa, clearly enjoying every bite.

That night, Rishab burns the midnight oil, eyes locked onto the glow of his laptop screen, chasing clarity through the chaos. But with the break of dawn, something shifts. The rising sun spills golden light into his room, bringing with it a quiet but powerful surge of hope. He wakes earlier than usual, drawn by a strange calm. Stepping into the garden, barefoot on the dewy grass, he breathes in the fresh morning air and picks up the day's newspaper. A hot cup of coffee warms his hands as he scans the headlines—not out of habit, but with renewed purpose. By 8:00 AM, he's at the breakfast table, focused. By 9:00, he's out the door—ready to face the world with something in his stride that wasn't there before.

MIL - EXECUTIVE FLOOR

Rishab enters Mallik's cabin.

RISHAB

"Mr. Mallik, I spoke to Haruto Ki this morning. He's available in the next hour to review the plan with us. Let's meet in the conference room."

Mallik is both surprised and pleased to see Rishab taking charge.

MEETING – LATER

In the meeting, Rishab successfully convinces Haruto Ki and the JMC executive team, securing more time to build the infrastructure for the JMC project. The executives are impressed with Rishab's detailed project plan and place their trust in him.

RISHAB'S OFFICE – OVER THE NEXT FEW DAYS

In the coming days, Rishab dedicates significant time to reviewing critical milestones for the JMC project. He prioritizes urgent tasks and works closely with his teams and vendors to meet these milestones.

He chairs daily standup meetings with both management and technical teams, reviewing the status of each task and resolving issues as they arise.

Rishab brings together the engineering teams and work supervisors in the boardroom to brainstorm and discuss on process improvements and efficiency. He collaborates with the Human resource team to expand the workforce on the production floor.

He ensures the teams work seamlessly across the board to achieve the key objectives for the project. Rishab works tirelessly day and night with his team to get all projects back on track. In a few months, the derailed projects are back on schedule, and the delivery dates are met.

Once a red KANBAN board at the PMO is now fully green, reflecting the team's hard work and dedication. However, the work pressure has taken a toll on Rishab's health.

MIL - STANDUP MEETING – MONDAY MORNING

During a routine Monday morning standup with his team, Rishab suddenly collapses, falling unconscious to the floor as panic erupts in the room. He is rushed to the hospital, where doctors reveal that dangerously high blood pressure is to blame and order him to take a week of complete rest.

Though Rishab stays home, after a couple of days, he becomes restless. He's eager to return to work, but Sujatha insists he stay home until he finishes his medication.

On the third day of his break, Rishab leaves early in the morning and heads to Karnunya.

He joins the cooks eagerly helping to prepare breakfast for the inmates. Despite his condition, he joyfully lifts a large vessel filled with the morning's breakfast and carries it from the kitchen to the dining area, his face glowing with satisfaction.

KARUNYA – MORNING

Chethana arrives by breakfast time, with her father dropping her off that morning.

Chethana is surprised to see Rishab laying out plates and serving breakfast to the inmates. He looks happy, smiling warmly as he serves. Rishab notices Chethana entering the dining area and walks towards her.

RISHAB

"I'm on a break from work for a week, so I thought I'd spend some time with the inmates."

CHETHANA

(smiling)

"That's a great!"

Just then, Gupta walks into the dining area, looking around for Chethana.

RISHAB

(surprised)

"Guptaji! What brings you here?"

GUPTA

"Good morning, sir. I came to hand over the house keys to Chethana. I'll be working late today as my team is installing the robotic arm at the production floor."

CHETHANA

"Rishab, he's my father."

Rishab is taken aback by the revelation. He goes close to Gupta.

RISHAB

(emotional)

"Guptaji, you stood shoulder to shoulder with my father during his toughest days. And now, Chethana is helping with Karunya. Our family is truly grateful to both of you. I can't express how much it means to me."

He steps forward and embraces Gupta.

GUPTA

"It's my duty and I'm proud that my daughter is fulfilling hers too."

KARUNYA GARDEN

After breakfast, Rishab and Chethana walk through the garden.

RISHAB

"Papa always supported me in everything I wanted to do in life. He was there for me in both my failures and my successes. Whether it was the employees at our company or the inmates here at Karunya, he wanted me to take care of them in his absence. I'm doing my best to fill that void. I know he's watching over me."

RISHAB
(CONT'D)

"He also wanted me to win the Championship. Unfortunately, that wish of his will remain unfulfilled."

Chethana gently rubs Rishab's shoulder, showing quiet compassion.

RISHAB

"Chethana, I have a surprise planned for Hunger Warriors. Can you join me this Saturday morning?"

CHETHANA

"Of course. What's the surprise?"

RISHAB (smiling)

"Wait until Saturday."

HW OFFICE – SATURDAY MORNING

Rishab stands beside a brand-new mini van, keys in hand, as Madan and Shyam approach. The van is branded with the Hunger Warriors logo and a message that reads: "Serving with Heart."

RISHAB

"This van is for you to help make your mission a little easier. I've seen the impact you're making, and I just wanted to be a part of it in some way."

Madan and Shyam are stunned for a moment, then step forward with wide smiles.

MADAN

"Rishab... this means the world to us. We've been struggling to keep up with the demand."

SHYAM

"Now we can reach more people, faster. Thank you from the bottom of our hearts."

They each hug Rishab tightly. Rishab, overwhelmed, tries to hold back his emotions.

RISHAB

(softly)

"This is what my father would've wanted. Helping people, that's what Karunya stands for."

Chethana stands a few steps away, smiling gently as she watches the moment. She sees Rishab's eyes glisten with unshed tears.

CHETHANA

(softly, to herself)

"He's truly carrying forward his father's legacy."

Rishab turns toward her, meeting her gaze. They exchange a quiet, meaningful smile.

R.S. NAGAR – LATE EVENING

It's Sunday. Rishab joins the Hunger Warriors to distribute food to the destitute in the R.S. Nagar area, about 25 kilometers from the Capital city.

Chethana and Rocket accompany too. They travel in the Hunger Warriors' van, loaded with food packets.

The van reaches its destination. The Hunger Warriors begin scanning the area for people in need. They spot half a dozen individuals sleeping on the pavement. There are no streetlights, but many have covered their faces to shield themselves from the bright moonlight flooding the street.

The Hunger Warriors climb down and begin unloading food packets. Rishab and Chethana also grab a few and start walking with them. An excited Rocket barks joyfully, trotting beside Rishab. His barking wakes several people.

The destitute slowly rise, squinting at the strangers. Among them are women, a few children and some elderly individuals. Rishab bends over slowly and offers a packet to a hesitant child. The boy glances at his mother, who nods silently. The child accepts the packet with a shy smile.

Rishab smiles back, takes more packets from Chethana and continues distributing them. Suddenly, someone rushes up, snatches a packet from Rishab's hand and shoves him aside.

Caught off guard, Rishab stumbles and falls hard onto the pavement. The remaining packets scatter from his hands. A large, disheveled man with long hair and a beard wearing ragged clothes growls as he scoops up the fallen packets. Without another word, the man darts away into the shadows. Rocket barks furiously and dashes after him. Chethana, Madan, and Shyam rush to Rishab.

Chethana quickly grabs Rishab's hand and help him to his feet.

CHETHANA

(panicked)

"Rishab, are you okay?"

Rishab straightens up, gripping his crutches to regain balance. His hand is bleeding, his finger injured in the fall.

With trembling hands, Chethana tears a strip from her dupatta and gently wraps it around Rishab's injured finger, her eyes filled with worry and unspoken care.

A concerned elderly man from the group approaches Rishab.

OLD MAN
"Sir, are you alright? I'm sorry... he's a madman. No one can control him."

Rocket returns, whimpering and licking Rishab's foot, trying to comfort him.

MALHOTRA HOME – NIGHT
Rishab lies in bed, unable to sleep. His mind replays the incident in R.S. Nagar - the chaos, the gratitude in the child's eyes, and Chethana's care.

He stares at the ceiling, his thoughts tangled in emotion —pain, compassion and a quiet realization of how much Chethana means to him.

MAHATMA GANDHI ROAD – MORNING
The city hums with the familiar bustle of a weekday morning. Rishab, sharp in his tailored suit, sits calmly in the back seat of a moving car, eyes scanning the world outside.

He notices Cpt. Chatterjee struggling with an old blue Lambretta scooter on the roadside. The scooter coughs, stutters, then falls silent. Chatterjee wipes sweat from his brow, frustration flickering across his kind, weathered face.

RISHAB
(to the driver)
"Stop the car."

As the car slows, Rishab opens the door. Rajeev Kumar, his ever-alert personal secretary, immediately gets out from the front passenger seat, sensing something is up.

RAJEEV KUMAR
(firm but respectful)
"Sir, why are you getting down? Just tell me what you need

and I'll take care of it."
RISHAB
(smiling slightly, eyes still on Chatterjee)
"That man..he is my friend. I need to see him."
Rishab steps out of the car. Rajeev hesitates, then follows. There's a quiet sense of duty in his steps.

Across the street Cpt. Chatterjee squints in the sunlight. Recognition dawns slowly, then joyfully across his face. He grins, arms opening wide.
Cpt. CHATTERJEE
"Rishab, my boy!"
They embrace, a warm, unspoken bond rekindled in the middle of the busy street.
RISHAB
"Sir, what happened? Is this your scooter?"
Cpt. CHATTERJEE
(grinning, pats the scooter)
"Yes! This is my loyal companion. A 1970 model Lambretta."
Cpt. CHATTERJEE
(sighs, fondly)
"Was on my way to Karunya and the old fellow gave up halfway."
RISHAB
(sympathetic)
"You can leave it here. I'll drop you off."
MR. CHATTERJEE
(grateful, but practical)
"Thank you, son. But we need to get him to the garage first. Only one mechanic around here knows how to treat this old-timer."
RISHAB

(nods)
"Of course, sir. I'll get it done."
He turns to Rajeev, who looks increasingly wary.
RISHAB
"Rajeev, can you take this scooter to the mechanic?"
RAJEEV KUMAR
(uncertain, eyeing the scooter)
"But... I... sir, it's not even starting..."
RISHAB
(gently firm)
"Please."
A brief pause. Rajeev sighs internally, then nods with reluctant resolve.
RAJEEV KUMAR
"Sure... sir. No worries. I'll handle it."
Cpt. CHATTERJEE
(chuckling)
"The workshop is just a kilometer away — straight road. Look for Salim's Garage on the left."
RAJEEV KUMAR
(slightly winded already)
"Got it, sir..."
Rishab and Cpt. Chatterjee step into the car, their conversation continuing as the door closes and the vehicle drives off.

Left behind, Rajeev Kumar, short and stout, stares at the silent scooter like it's a sleeping beast. He sighs again, adjusts his sleeves and with visible effort, rolls it off its stand. The scooter creaks.

As he begins pushing it down the road, he mutters under his breath, beads of sweat already forming.
SALIM'S GARAGE

Rishab and Cpt. Chatterjee arrive at the workshop within ten minutes. Chatterjee gets down first and gestures for Rishab to join him.

Salim, working inside the garage, steps out with a big smile upon seeing Cpt. Chatterjee.

SALIM

"Hello, Dada! How are you? Where's your scooter?"

Cpt. CHATTERJEE

"It's coming right behind us. Seems to have a starting issue."

Just then, Rishab walks up to them. Salim eyes him curiously.

Cpt. CHATTERJEE

"Salim, this is Rishab."

Salim's expression shifts. Recognition dawns and he rushes forward to greet Rishab, holding his hands with admiration.

SALIM

(excited)

"Sir! I can't believe you're here..in my garage. I'm a huge fan!"

Salim's joy fades slightly as he remembers Rishab's accident. His tone turns more heartfelt.

SALIM

(softly)

"You are my superhero."

Rishab smiles, touched by the sentiment.

Cpt. CHATTERJEE

"Rishab, Salim is one of the most well-known mechanics around here. He's an expert in servicing all kinds of motorcycles."

RISHAB

(smiling)

"Good to know."

As Rishab peers into the garage, something catches his eye. He slowly walks in and spots a motorcycle chassis sitting on a workbench.

RISHAB

(curious)

"Are you building a motorcycle?"

SALIM

(humbly)

"Yes, sir...trying to build a Harley-Davidson for myself."

RISHAB

"Hmm...Harley-Davidson? That's interesting."

Rishab notices photos of Harley-Davidsons pinned up across the walls — vintage models, Road Kings, and custom builds.

RISHAB

"So you're a Harley fan?"

SALIM

"Yes, sir...since childhood. I'm trying to build a Road King."

Rishab steps closer, examining the frame with a sharp, technical eye.

RISHAB

"I see some welding issues here. Also joints need better finishing."

SALIM

"Sir, I'm trying to fit the engine, but the frame doesn't align properly."

RISHAB

"Yeah...the dimensions are off. We'll need to rework the chassis."

Cpt. CHATTERJEE

"Salim, Rishab isn't just a racer, he's an automobile

engineer and runs his own company."

RISHAB

"Salim, can I help you build your Road King?"

Salim is stunned, then beams with joy.

SALIM

"Of course, sir! I'd be honored!"

At that moment, Rajeev arrives at the garage, completely drenched in sweat, panting heavily. He's pushed the scooter all the way.

RAJEEV KUMAR

"Sir... your scooter..."

Salim rushes forward and takes over. Cpt. Chatterjee thanks Rajeev with a pat on the back.

Inside the garage, Rishab is rolling up his sleeves, already focused.

RISHAB

"Come on, Salim. Let's fix the frame and check if the engine fits."

Salim eagerly joins him. Rishab takes the measuring tape, examines the structure, and starts sketching a blueprint on paper.

He begins the welding himself, sparks flying as he works completely engrossed. The oil stains his hands and a layer of dust from the work floor clings to his shirt, leaving visible smudges.

Outside, Rajeev waits patiently.

By evening, the engine is successfully mounted onto the modified chassis.

SALIM

(overjoyed)

"Sir...you're a genius! I've been stuck on this for ten days!"

RISHAB

"No worries bro..anytime! but your Road King will need a

more powerful engine. Let's go for a 500cc. I'll arrange for the engine."

Rishab stands in the garage grease-covered but smiling, visibly content with the day's efforts.

MONTAGE – DAYS PASSING

Everyday after office hours, Rishab returns to Salim's garage, the two work late into the night—often till **1 AM**.

Rishab sketches designs, welds and works on the gear assembly. The chassis, gear sprocket and the drive train are completed within a week. During this time a deep friendship blossoms between Rishab and Salim.

Rishab, once withdrawn, now finds joy and renewed energy in this shared purpose.

SALIM'S GARAGE – NIGHT

Rishab is hunched over an iPad, reviewing shock absorber specs. At the same time, he talks through fitting details with Salim. But Salim seems distant and restless. Rishab notices.

RISHAB

"Salim, you okay?"

SALIM

(low tone)

"I'm fine, sir..."

RISHAB

"You sure? Feels like something's on your mind."

SALIM

(hesitant)

"Sir... can we take a break tomorrow? I have some personal work."

RISHAB

"Sure, no worries. Let's catch up the day after."

SALIM

"Sure, sir."

Rishab walks over to the tap and washes his hands. Salim follows, quieter now, more relaxed.

SALIM

"Sir, it's my first wedding anniversary tomorrow. I'm planning to take Rahima out for dinner."

RISHAB

(smiling)

"Wow... Congratulations, Salim."

SALIM

"Thanks"

RISHAB

(continues washing his hands)

"If I may ask... was it a love marriage or an arranged one?"

SALIM

(with a smile)

"Sir, it was one-way love at first."

RISHAB

"Hmm. Who was on the one-way street?"

SALIM

"Sir... you really want to hear my story?"

Rishab looks around and notices a small stone compartment. He walks over and sits down.

RISHAB

"Sure, I'm ready."

Salim sits beside him and begins to narrate his love story.

CUT TO FLASHBACK:

SALIM'S Garage – DAY

Salim is busy attending to a customer's complaint when he notices a beautiful girl walking down the street. His eyes follow her — captivated.

SALIM

"Sir... whenever I see Rahima, my heart melts and words

get stuck in my throat. We studied in the same school. But I had to drop out — I wasn't interested in studies. I joined my father and started working in the garage. I had my first crush on her back in primary school.

Even though we lived in the same colony, I never had the courage to express my feelings. Her father passed away four years ago due to illness. The family lost everything during his treatment."

SALIM'S GARAGE – NIGHT – 10 PM

Salim is working late. The hum of tools fades as a voice calls out from the entrance. He looks up, surprised. It's Rahima and she looks tense and worried.

Salim's heart pounds.

SALIM

"Rahima...what happened?"

RAHIMA

"Salim, Ammi is not feeling well. I need help getting her to the hospital."

CUT TO PRESENT:

SALIM'S GARAGE

SALIM

"Rahima's mother was a very pious and hardworking woman. She worked day and night for her daughter's future. She was a tailor at a nearby garment factory. On top of that, she used to take stitching orders from home at night. She was an asthma patient and that night, her condition worsened. The years of hard work and constant exposure to dust had made asthma her constant companion."

CUT TO FLASHBACK:

RAHIMA

"Is there a taxi you can call? Or maybe book one from your phone?"

Salim pulls out an old basic phone from his pocket, disheartened. However he notices Rahima also holding the same model.

SALIM

"Don't worry. Let me check if I can find an auto rickshaw or a taxi nearby."

RAHIMA

(tense, with tears rolling down)

"Please... she's struggling to breathe. We can't wait any longer."

SALIM

"There's one way we can get her to the hospital quickly."

FLASHBACK CONTINUES:

CITY ROADS – NIGHT

A dusty, dimly-lit street. Salim rides his motorcycle with urgency. Rahima sits behind him, holding her unconscious mother tightly. Her eyes are filled with fear, her arms wrapped protectively around her mother.

SALIM

"I took Rahima's mother to the hospital on my motorcycle. Rahima was sitting behind me, holding her mother tightly."

GOVERNMENT HOSPITAL – NIGHT

Salim rushes into the emergency entrance with Rahima and her mother. A nurse takes over. Moments later, a DOCTOR walks out with a grim face. Rahima breaks down in tears.

SALIM

"What more could I ask for? It felt like I was saving her whole world that night. But unfortunately, it was too late. Rahima's mother took her last breath at the government hospital,just after being admitted."

CREMATORIUM– DAY

A small group gathers for the funeral. Rahima stands silently, eyes swollen, face numb. Salim stands beside her, a quiet pillar of strength.

SALIM

"Rahima was now all alone. She had no one left. I stood by her side until the final rites were completed. The very next day, I spoke to my Abba about Rahima."

BACK TO PRESENT:

SALIM

"I can't believe it's already been a year... time truly flies. She's the brightest light in my life — an incredible wife to me and a devoted daughter to my father. We're so lucky to have her."

Salim and Rishab sit on the stone ledge, the sounds of distant traffic and crickets in the background. Rishab looks at Salim, visibly moved.

RISHAB

"That's beyond beautiful, Salim! You held Rahima's world from falling apart."

Salim smiles humbly, eyes lowered.

SALIM

"Life taught me more than school ever could, Sir."

They sit in silence for a moment, the weight of the story settling between them.

RISHAB

(smiling)

"Well, go celebrate your anniversary tomorrow. You've earned it."

SALIM

(with gratitude)

"Thanks, Sir."

They both rise. Salim switches off the garage lights as they walk out together into the night.

SALIM'S HOME – THE NEXT DAY – EVENING

Salim is getting ready. He's wearing his best outfit. Rahima looks stunning in a traditional salwar suit. Salim looks at her with admiration, gently holding her chin.

SALIM

(softly, looking into her eyes)

"Rahima, when I look at you tonight, it feels like the moon itself has left the sky and come home to me."

Rahima blushes and wraps her arms around him in a warm hug. Just then, Salim's phone rings. He answers.

RISHAB

(on phone)

"Happy anniversary, Salim. Please convey my wishes to Rahima too."

SALIM

"Thanks, Sir."

RISHAB

"There's a car waiting outside to take you both for your anniversary dinner."

Salim, surprised, steps toward the window.

SALIM

"Sir...?"

He quickly walks out of the house. Outside, a sleek car is parked and a uniformed chauffeur walks up to him.

CHAUFFEUR

"Sir, the car is ready."

Salim lifts the phone back to his ear.

RISHAB

"Enjoy your evening my friend!!"

The call ends. Salim stands still for a moment, touched.

SALIM

(joyful tone)

"Thanks, sir!!!"

He turns to Rahima, smiling. The chauffeur opens the door. They both step into the car.

CITY STREETS – LATE EVENING

The car glides through the city, lights reflecting off its windows, carrying Salim and Rahima toward one of the city's most famous seven-star hotels.

THE GRAND HOTEL – RECEPTION AREA

Salim and Rahima enter the luxurious lobby, greeted by a soft elegant melody playing in the background. The staff offers them a warm, heartfelt welcome. One of the attendants presents them with a bouquet of fresh flowers and Rahima's face lights up as she takes it, holding it gently to her chest. The couple is guided through the lavish lobby, treated like royalty.

As they walk to their table, the soft glow of candles flickers across the room. Their table, set in a quiet corner, offers a breathtaking view of the city skyline. The restaurant staff pulls out chairs for them and offers a final respectful nod before stepping away.

They sit, a soft, intimate silence filling the space between them. The flickering candlelight casts gentle shadows on their faces as they share a delicious, romantic dinner, exchanging smiles and laughter. The time seems to slow down as they savour the moment, lost in each other's presence.

SALIM'S GARAGE – MORNING

Salim is focused on working with a metal sheet for his dream bike when he notices Rishab entering the garage. As soon as Salim sees him, he quickly walks over and gives him a tight hug.

SALIM

(overwhelmed)

"Sir, thank you so much for yesterday's treat. I never imagined I'd even have a glass of water in a place like that and yet, you gave Rahima and me an evening we'll never forget."

RISHAB

"I'm happy both of you enjoyed the most precious day of your life."

Rishab smiles and continues...

RISHAB

"Come on, buddy, let's assemble the engine today. I've skipped office to get this completed."

Salim's eyes fill with tears, his emotions taking over.

SALIM

"I don't understand...Why are you doing all this for me? What did I do to deserve it?"

RISHAB

(with sincerity, his voice soft but unwavering)

"I'm not doing this *for* you, Salim. I'm doing it because I need to. Thank you for letting me into your life, for giving me a place in your world. That's a gift I'll never take for granted."

Rishab walks over to the work area and retrieves the spare parts from the box, placing them onto the table. Salim rushes in to help.

It's a long day for both Rishab and Salim. Together, they successfully assemble the new 500cc engine, mount it onto the frame and test its functionality.

They continue fitting the front and rear shock absorbers and by evening they've completed 60 percent of the work.

In the coming days, Rishab works extensively in refining the motorcycle's design while Salim focuses on the fabrication according to the design specifications.

They complete the assembly of the rolling chassis which includes the frame, rake, wheels, brakes, and fenders. The exhaust system is set up and the transmission is successfully tested.

They finish the build by installing the seat and mock up the bike with mirrors and lights. The motorcycle is now ready for painting. Salim pushes the bike to the painting area.

SALIM

(excited)

"Sir, I'll finish the painting tonight and we'll have our first ride tomorrow!"

RISHAB

(smiling)

"Sure, Salim. I'll be here by 5 PM tomorrow."

Both bid each other goodbye and Rishab quickly rushes back to his car, heading home. Salim stays behind in the garage, absorbed in his work.

He spends the entire night and the following day painting the bike, meticulously adding the final touches. By evening, Salim is filled with excitement, eagerly awaiting Rishab's arrival.

He can't wait to show him the result of their hard work — his dream now realized.

But as the evening passes, Rishab doesn't show up. Salim waits... but he doesn't come. The next four days drag on and still, Rishab doesn't visit. Salim tries calling him multiple times but each call goes unanswered.

SALIM'S GARAGE – EVENING

Salim is working on a customer's scooter when he notices Rishab standing at the entrance of the garage.

SALIM

(in a happy tone)

"Sir... I've been waiting for you all this while. Come inside, our bike is ready."

Rishab walks into the work area and find the motorcycle covered with a blanket. Salim steps forward and pulls it off, revealing a roughly Harley-Davidson Road King – style motorcycle gleaming on the platform.

Rishab gives Salim a hug.

RISHAB

(beaming with pride)

"Now that's a masterpiece!"

He circles the bike, eyes gleaming as he takes in every detail like a collector admiring rare art.

Salim rolls the bike off the platform, the polished metal catching the light. Outside, he swings a leg over and turns the key — **VROOOOM!**

The engine growls to life, loud and powerful. Rishab laughs, electrified.

RISHAB

"That sound... it's alive!"

SALIM

"Come on sir, let's go."

Rishab slowly climbs onto the motorcycle and holds Salim tightly from behind. Salim accelerates with caution.

RISHAB

"Hey Salim, give it a full throttle. Let's see what this bike can do."

SALIM

(in an excited tone)
"Sure, Sir — here we go..."
Salim twists the throttle and the bike zooms off. With a 500cc engine, the motorcycle produced 43.5 horsepower and rivals many modern bikes on the road. They take a right turn onto the highway. The two men ride their self-made motorcycle, cutting through the wind — it's truly a great ride.

They stop the bike on a bridge to enjoy the beautiful sunset. Both watch the sun dip below the horizon, taking with it the vibrant reds and oranges it had painted across the sky before disappearing behind the mountains. It's a splendid view.

SALIM
"Sir...can I ask you something?"
RISHAB
"Of course, buddy."
SALIM
(quiet, sincere)
"I want to see you race again."
RISHAB
(laughs bitterly, sarcastic)
"Are you serious? I can't even hold a motorcycle these days, let alone race one."
SALIM
(firm tone)
"You're still the Moto2 champion. No one's touched your record, not even close."
SALIM
(continuing, emotion rising)
"I know it in my heart — you still have it in you. The fire, the fight! The finish line's still out there, waiting for you, Sir!"

RISHAB
(turns away, voice cold)
"Let it wait. That chapter is over."
SALIM
(softly)
"Only if you say it is."
Long pause. The wind blows softly in the silence.
RISHAB
(changing the subject, avoiding)
"Come on...let's go. It's getting late."
Rishab walks toward the bike. Salim watches him for a moment, then quietly joins him.
SALIM'S GARAGE – NIGHT
The bike comes to a gentle stop outside the garage. The engine cuts. Silence. Rishab slowly gets off the motorcycle, still caught in the moment. Salim jumps off and carefully sets it on the center stand.

A brief pause. They share a quiet smile under the dim garage lights.
RISHAB
"Thank you, Salim. That was more than just a ride."
SALIM
(eyes shining, voice soft)
"I'm the one who should thank you. You made this possible. You didn't just build a bike with me sir — you brought my dream to life."
Rishab looks at the bike, then back at Salim.
RISHAB
"Can I ask you something? And I need an honest answer."
SALIM
(confused, curious)
"Sir...? What is it?"
RISHAB

(quietly)

"Can I have this bike?"

Salim is stunned for a moment...then a slow, emotional smile spreads across his face.

SALIM

(softly, with warmth)

"Sir, this bike? It's already yours."

RISHAB

(smiles back)

"Then bring it to my office tomorrow morning."

They nod, a silent agreement between brothers, not by blood but by bond.

As Rishab turns and walks toward his car, Salim watches him go, his eyes misty.

SALIM

(to himself, voice trembling with emotion)

"I'd give my life for you, Sir...What's a bike compared to that?"

MIL RECEPTION AREA – MORNING

Salim rides the motorcycle up to Rishab's office. At the gate, a security guard signals him to park near the entrance. Salim parks the bike carefully and walks toward the reception area. He pauses at the front desk.

SALIM

"Madam, I'm here to hand over the motorcycle to sir. Could you please let him know I've arrived?"

RECEPTIONIST

(slightly puzzled)

"Sir...?"

SALIM (realizing)

"Oh—sorry, I mean Rishab sir."

RECEPTIONIST
(with a friendly smile)
"Of course. Please have a seat, sir."

Salim glances around and notices a plush sofa in the lounge. He walks toward it, but hesitates before sitting down. This is his first time in such a corporate setting. He stands awkwardly, taking in the surroundings, visibly anxious.

Just then, Salim turns and sees Rishab approaching.

RISHAB
"Sorry to keep you waiting, Salim. I was caught up in a meeting."

SALIM
"No problem, Sir..."

RISHAB
"Thanks, bro. Shall we go?"

SALIM
(Inquisitive tone)
"Where to Sir?"

RISHAB
(Smiling)
"Come with me."

Rishab leads Salim through the office. They walk across the production floor, pass the warehouse and take a right turn toward the garage.

MIL – GARAGE AREA

Both men walk into the garage. The lights are dim, casting shadows across the space. The atmosphere is heavy with anticipation. Rishab walks to the corner of the garage and flicks a switch. The lights slowly flicker on, revealing the full expanse of the garage.

Salim's eyes are drawn to something in the center of the room, a large object covered with a red cloth. His heart beats faster as he stares at it.

Rishab turns to Salim, locking eyes with him, then takes his hand. They share a quiet moment and Salim feels a lump in his throat.

RISHAB

"Come with me."

Rishab pulls Salim toward the covered object. There's a quiet pause, an electric silence between them. He releases Salim's hand and steps closer to the object. With deliberate care, he pulls the cloth away.

The motorcycle is revealed. A brand new Harley Davidson Road King, gleaming under the lights. The real HD ROAD KING!! It's almost too much for Salim to comprehend.

RISHAB

(his voice barely above a whisper)

"Salim...This is yours."

Salim stands frozen, his entire body still. His heart races, but his legs feel as though they're rooted to the ground. The sight of the bike, his dream, is almost too overwhelming.

RISHAB

(gently)

"Come, take a look at it."

Salim remains motionless for a moment longer, then slowly steps forward. His eyes flicker with disbelief as he walks around the bike, his hands trembling as they hover over the smooth surface.

SALIM

(in awe, voice cracking)

"Sir... this... this is beyond anything I could ever imagine. It's... too costly. How can I take this?"

Rishab steps closer, his eyes softening, his voice filled with deep sincerity.

RISHAB
(emotion thick in his voice)
"Not costlier than your friendship."

Salim's eyes glisten with tears, his heart overflowing with emotion. Without a word, Salim pulls Rishab into a tight embrace, his gratitude and love for his friend pouring out in that simple act.

Rishab smiles, his eyes misting just slightly as he pats Salim on the back.

RISHAB
"Come on...Let me show you the controls."

Salim nods, still in disbelief, but as Rishab explain the bike's features, Salim listens intently, absorbing every word. The bond between them is palpable.

Finally, Salim sits on the bike, his hands shaking as he turns the key. The engine roars to life, a powerful, guttural sound that echoes in the garage.

RISHAB
(his voice filled with excitement and pride)
"Go ahead, Bro. Take it for a spin."

A surge of adrenaline courses through Salim. He grips the handlebars, his heart pounding as he feels the power of the bike beneath him. The wind rushes around him as he accelerates, the world blurring around him. He rides freely, completely immersed in the moment, his dream finally realized.

Rishab stands at the garage entrance, watching his friend ride. A proud smile tugs at the corner of his lips. His heart swells as he watches Salim, his brother...live the dream he always deserved.

MIL - RECEPTION AREA – LATER THAT DAY.
Rishab and Salim stand side by side, their eyes fixed on the motorcycle they built together. The bike is now

suspended from the ceiling, hanging proudly in the reception area of Malhotra Industries.

The custom built HD Road King, glistening in the light, is a testament to their hard work, passion and unbreakable bond. The sight of it, suspended in mid-air, almost feels like a dream made real.

Rishab, standing just a few feet away, watches the motorcycle with a quiet sense of pride. This wasn't just a bike — It is the culmination of everything they had fought for, every challenge they had overcome together.

For Rishab, this bike wasn't just a machine, it was a symbol of **New Life**, **Hope**, **Teamwork**, and most of all, **True Friendship**.

SALIM

(his voice full of emotion)

"Thank you, sir."

Rishab turns to Salim, a soft smile spreading across his face. The word "sir" are foreign coming from Salim, and it strikes a chord deep within him.

RISHAB

(softly, with deep warmth)

"Please... don't call me "sir." You're my brother. You always have been and you always will be..."

Salim looks at Rishab, his eyes filled with gratitude and love. They don't need words to say what's in their hearts. This motorcycle, this moment, it represents everything they've been through together....

❧❧❧

MIL - RISHAB'S CABIN– MORNING

Rishab receives an email from FMSCI. It's an invitation to the Tiger Racing Team launch event on Saturday, the team that will represent India in the British MotoGP

Championship.

Rishab decides to attend the launch party.

TAJ HOTEL – EVENING

A huge stage is set up with a large screen displaying the BTM motorcycle and the members of the Tiger Racing Team.

Prominent guests from the racing fraternity, businessmen, film stars, international sponsors, FMSCI officials and members of the press are present at the launch party.

Rishab walks into the arena and takes a seat in one of the back rows, maintaining a low profile.

The Tiger Racing Team is introduced to the audience, followed by the grand unveiling of the BTM motorcycle. Vinod enters in full racing gear and waves to the crowd. The audience cheers enthusiastically.

The screen behind plays Vinod's journey to the World Championship — but it notably omits his loss to Rishab in the Moto2 Championship.

The representatives from the sponsor companies take turns speaking about their association with the Tiger Racing Team and Vinod. The FMSCI President, Behera, takes the stage for the closing speech. He praises Vinod's impressive performance in the preliminary and qualifying stages and wishes him best of luck for the championship. Behera also confirms that an elite international coaching team has been arranged to help Vinod excel.

Behera then opens a bottle of champagne to toast the Tiger Racing team and wish them success.

Rishab watches the proceedings silently, feeling hurt that his own community in the racing world has seemingly forgotten him. Many dignitaries ignore him, and some even avoid speaking to him.

After the presentation, the press surrounds Vinod for interviews. The arena features a lavish spread of food and drinks. As guests begin moving toward the dining area, Rishab quietly walks to the bar, picks up a drink and settles into a corner of the hall.

Vinod spots Rishab. He excuses himself from the press and walks toward him.

VINOD
(cocky, with a smirk)
"Well, well...Rishab, didn't expect to see you here."

RISHAB
(controlled, sincere)
"Congratulations, Vinod."

VINOD
(pointing proudly at the BTM motorcycle)
"That red beast..., I'm going to dominate on it. Alessandro and Martin ? They better move aside."

RISHAB
(calm, but pointed)
"If you sharpen your cornering, you just might. Right now, it's still your weakest link."

Vinod freezes, ego bruised. The smile fades. His tone darkens.

VINOD
(cold, offended)
"And who the hell are you to talk about my technique?"

RISHAB
(evenly)
"Someone who beat you, because of that very flaw. I'm just telling you what no one else will — fix it. Or you'll crash before the finish line."

Silence. Vinod's jaw tightens. His pride wounded, his voice now a growl.

VINOD

(furious)

"You don't get to lecture me. Not anymore. Look at you... where do you stand today..?"

RISHAB

(quiet, firm)

"Also fix your attitude. Or it'll be the thing that ends you, not the competition."

Vinod snaps. rage overcomes him. He lunges forward, grabs Rishab by the collar and slams him against the wall. The room blurs for Rishab as the breath is knocked out of him. He gasps, struggling. A few heads turn. Bharadwaj rushes over.

BHARADWAJ

(alarmed)

"Hey! What's going on here?"

Vinod pauses, his chest heaving. Slowly, he loosens his grip, but his venom remains.

VINOD

(mocking)

"You've put on weight, you should take your own advice, get back in shape buddy..."

Vinod throws one last glare, then walks away into the crowd.

The celebration resumes, but the moment lingers.

Rishab straightens himself. His hands tremble slightly. He doesn't speak, eyes glassy, he turns and walks out, the sounds of laughter behind him echoing like a taunt.

Bharadwaj watches from the entrance, still, silent as Rishab limps toward the parking lot, swallowed by the night.

RISHAB'S HOME – NIGHT – GARAGE

Rishab opens the garage door and steps inside. He walks slowly toward his XTR 1000 motorcycle. The bike is blanketed in dust. He blows gently on the tank, revealing a glimpse of its once -glorious run. His hand glides over the metal, lingering.

This is the very motorcycle he was meant to ride at the MotoGP World Championship.

His eyes well up. The heaviness of lost dreams crashes over him. Rishab drops to his knees beside the bike, overcome with grief.

RISHAB'S BEDROOM – LATE NIGHT

Rishab jolts awake, breathless, haunted. A vivid dream — the final moments of his father's life still echoes in his mind. Rishab is shivering, drenched in sweat. He stumbles out of bed and into the washroom.

He stares at himself in the mirror — eyes red, jaw clenched, breath ragged. He splashes water on his face, again and again, until his hands begin to steady. Slowly, he regains control.

Wrapped in silence, Rishab steps onto the balcony. He gazes at the sky — vast, still, endless. He doesn't return to bed. He just stands there, watching, thinking, remembering.
Alone with the stars... and the weight of everything left unsaid.

RISHAB'S HOME – MORNING

The early morning light filters through as Rishab, dressed in a tracksuit, steps into his personal gym on the terrace. He walks to the corner where dumbbells lie neatly arranged. He picks up two five-pound weights and begins curling them — slow, strained reps.

But even this light weight feels too heavy. His arms tremble. His body, once a machine now feels like it's betraying him. After just a few reps he gives up, breathless and frustrated.

He sets the dumbbells down, ashamed.

With quiet determination, Rishab turns to the treadmill. He climbs on steadying himself carefully. His finger hovers, then presses start. The deck begins to move at the lowest speed. Rishab tries to match the pace but struggles. His balance falters. His artificial limb isn't reacting fast enough.

Then — a slip. A loud **THUD** echoes across the terrace as Rishab crashes down, his head hitting the handle rail before he collapses onto the floor.

RISHAB'S ROOM – LATER

Blood trickles down from a gash on Rishab's forehead. The doctor finishes stitching the wound, three stitches in total and wraps a bandage around it.

DOCTOR

"Take a couple of days' rest. No strain."

Vivek nods and walks the doctor to the door. Sujatha sits beside her son, gently wiping the dried blood from his face. Her hands tremble. Her eyes don't blink.

RISHAB

(in a low, broken voice)

"Sorry, Maa... your tears never seem to dry because of me."

Sujatha says nothing. Her face quivers with pain, she leans down and gently kisses his bandaged forehead.

A silent, aching love — deeper than words.

RISHAB'S ROOM – EVENING

The room is dimly lit by the fading evening light. Rishab sits upright on his bed, wrapped in quiet intensity. Chethana sits across from him, sensing something has shifted in him.

RISHAB

(steady, resolute)

"I need to get back in shape. I have to race again."

Chethana blinks, caught off guard by the certainty in his voice.

RISHAB

(voice rising, eyes burning with determination)

"I have to hit the Silverstone race track. No matter what it takes."

CHETHANA

(softly, unsure)

"But...how?"

RISHAB

(exhaling, conflicted)

"I don't know. All I know is — I need strength. I need my body back. My mind back. If I'm going to ride again... I need to earn it."

CHAPTER FOUR

TRANSFORMATION

MONTAGE – RISHAB'S EFFORTS TO GET BACK INTO SHAPE ARE PAYING OFF

It is 5:00 AM. The alarm rings. Rishab rises. He takes slow, steady walks in and around the house. In his personal gym, he lifts light weights, pushing through pain. His reps are few. His breath is short. But his will — unshaken.

The weeks pass. The routine continues. Sweat drips. Muscles ache. Yet frustration brews. Rishab stares at himself in the mirror, gripping the sides of the sink. He doesn't see progress. The time is slipping through his fingers.

RISHAB

(to himself, frustrated)

"This isn't enough... I need more. I need to push harder."

He knows time is against him and Silverstone won't wait.

RISHAB'S BEDROOM

It's a quiet Sunday. The morning paper lies open on the coffee table. Rishab flips through it idly , then stops. His eyes widen. An ad for the **Delhi Half Marathon** stares back at him.

Front and center: a smiling **Sikh athlete** with a prosthetic blade — mid-stride, full of life.

Hope ignites. Rishab grabs his phone and dials Chethana.

SPLIT SCENE – INTERCUT PHONE CALL

CHETHANA

(excited, answering)

"Rishab! Did you see the ad?"

He pauses, stunned.

RISHAB

"You mean...the Delhi marathon?"

CHETHANA

"Yes! The man with the prosthetic, he's running! Can you believe that?"

RISHAB

(with renewed energy)

"Let's meet. Today. Afternoon?"

CHETHANA

"Done.!!"

They hang up. For the first time in weeks, Rishab smiles — faint, but real. A door has opened.

MALHOTRA'S HOME – BALCONY

Rishab and Chethana sit together in the balcony, the newspaper ad spread between them. A gentle breeze blows, but their focus is unwavering.

CHETHANA

(pointing at the ad, inspired)

"Look at this, Major Abhinav Singh. He's the face of this year's Delhi Marathon. A Kargil war hero!! Lost his leg...came back from the brink of death and became a symbol of hope for millions."

RISHAB

(softly, deeply moved)

"I read about him. His story...it's unbelievable. He didn't just survive — he ran marathons. He became the fighter."

CHETHANA
(scrolling her phone, holding it out)
"Oscar Pistorius. South African sprinter, competed in the 2012 Olympics with blades. He ran with champions. No excuses. Just belief."

Rishab takes the phone, eyes widening as he reads. Something shifts in him — a flicker of life returning.

RISHAB
(Awestruck)
"This is unreal!!"

CHETHANA
(gently, firmly)
"There are so many like them. People who didn't let their scars define them. Sudha Chandran, an actress, she danced on world stages with a prosthetic limb. Her spirit didn't break. Major D.P. Singh a brave soldier who beat death and sprung back to life and became a challenger."

Rishab falls silent. But his silence is not defeat — it's focus. A spark has caught flame. His heart swells with hope, eyes lit with a new fire.

MONTAGE – NIGHT INTO DAY

Rishab sits in front of his laptop, deeply engrossed, clicking through stories of para-athletes and amputee champions. The images flash across the screen: medals, blades, grit, triumph!!

He prints out articles, takes notes. watches videos. He studies Major Abhinav Singh's interviews like sacred text.

Rishab is no longer just dreaming — he's preparing.

NEW LIFE HEALTH SCIENCE & ROBOTICS – PROSTHETIC LAB

Rishab and Chethana sit across from Dr. Jagadish, a Senior Orthopedic and Prosthetic Limb Expert.

Dr. Jagadish examines Rishab with careful hands and compassionate eyes. Measurements. Scans. Moulds.

DR. JAGADISH

"We'll design something that works with your spirit — not just your body."

MONTAGE – RISHAB'S PROSTHETIC JOURNEY

Weeks pass. Rishab visits New Life regularly. The engineers and doctors work tirelessly.

A custom prosthetic limb takes shape — sleek, sturdy, built for motion.

NEW LIFE HOSPITAL – PHYSIOTHERAPY ROOM

A milestone moment.

Rishab, Chethana, and Sujatha stand in quiet anticipation. Rishab fits the prosthetic limb for the first time. Awkward. Unsteady. He hesitates.

But Chethana is at his side. Sujatha holds his hand.

CHEERFUL THERAPIST

"One step at a time, Mr. Rishab. You're not alone."

Rishab takes a shaky step... then another... and another. An hour later — he's walking.

MONTAGE – RISHAB TRAINS HARD:

Rishab trains daily. Slowly, he graduates to the prosthetic blade. The first run is painful and brutal.

His body jerks violently with every stride. His stump bruises & the hips scream. Sleepless nights, soaked bandages, gritted teeth, but Rishab never stops.

Every dawn, he's on the road. 10 kilometres. One goal. Then weight training at dusk.

He crafts his own routine — a mix of physiotherapy, strength training, and endurance runs. He adapts his diet.

Eats clean. Trains harder.

RISHAB'S GYM – EVENING

Rishab stares at himself in the mirror, not with doubt but pride. His body is lean. Muscles defined. Posture strong. He is no longer broken. He is rebuilt. Reforged!!

TRACK FIELD – SUNRISE

Rishab runs with power, his blade slicing through the air. Not limping. Not falling. Flying.

RISHAB'S BEDROOM – NIGHT

Rishab sits on the edge of his bed. He opens a drawer and pulls out an old newspaper, unfolding it with care. His eyes scan the page until they land on the **Delhi Half Marathon** advertisement.

He reads it slowly, absorbing every word — the date, the details, the challenge.

A moment of stillness, then with quiet resolve, he turns to his computer, powers it on and opens the marathon's registration page. His fingers hesitate for a moment...then begin typing.

Name. Age. Prosthetic runner. He hits **submit**. The event is scheduled for the coming Sunday.

A new countdown begins.

JAWAHARLAL NEHRU STADIUM – NEW DELHI – MORNING

The sun rises over the capital, casting a golden glow on over 20,000 runners gathered for the 21 KM Delhi Half Marathon. The atmosphere is electric — banners wave, cameras flash, hearts pound.

Among the sea of athletes, Rishab Malhotra walks into the stadium. Calm. Focused. Determined.

He collects his race pass from the reception and heads toward the starting line, blending into the crowd of runners. But not for long. He notices other blade runners. He isn't alone.

Then — whispers.

A few participants recognize him. Faces turn. Fingers point. A ripple of curiosity spreads.

Voice in the crowd

"Is that... Rishab Malhotra?"

Suddenly, the buzz becomes a wave. The runners and onlookers gather. Phones click. Questions fly.

And then — the press descends.

REPORTER

(shoving a mic forward)

"Rishab! Are you confident you can finish the race?"

Rishab's eyes shift. He's overwhelmed — no way out. The noise, the crowd, the flashing cameras.

He stands frozen, until a firm voice cuts through the chaos.

MAJOR ABHINAV SINGH

"Champ...just focus on the finish line."

Rishab turns. Major Abhinav Singh, decorated war hero and blade runner, stands before him - Smiling, Steady and Strong.

Rishab's eyes light up in admiration, gratitude, disbelief all at once.

RISHAB

(softly, humbled)

"Sir... thank you. You have no idea what you mean to me."

They clasp hands. No more words needed.

MARATHON STARTING POINT – MOMENTS LATER

The starting gun **fires.**

A tidal wave of runners surges forward. Among them, Rishab takes his first few steps — slow, deliberate. The course winds out of the stadium toward Jagannath temple, the crowd cheering along the barricades. After few kilometres, the blade under him jolts. Every stride is effort. Every second is pain. But he moves.

One by one, runners overtake him. The doubt creeps in, pain builds, eyes watch. The pedestrians, runners, spectators — their stares laced with sympathy, pity, and quiet skepticism.

But Rishab runs. Not to win. Not to prove a point. To answer a question that's haunted him since the accident: "Am I still enough?"

His legs ache. The stump burns. The blade pounds against the pavement, sending shockwaves through his body. But Rishab doesn't stop.

The Podium, NEAR RASHTRAPATI BHAVAN – HOURS LATER

The sun now sits high in the sky. The race is long over, trophies have been handed out. The crowds begin to leave.

Suddenly — a shout cuts through the chatter.

SOMEONE

"Here comes the blade runner!"

Heads turn. Gasps echo. A figure approaches from the distance — stumbling, exhausted, drenched in sweat. It's Rishab.

Major Abhinav Singh turns. A smile spreads across his face as he watches Rishab push forward inch by inch refusing to stop.

And then Rishab crosses the finish line. It has taken him four hours and twenty minutes to hit the final line.

He collapses to the ground, gasping, broken...but victorious.

The medical team rushes in, fanning him, offering water. But the sound that fills the air now isn't panic. It's applause!!

The runners, onlookers, media, all on their feet cheering, clapping, crying.

Major Abhinav Singh runs to him and pulls him into a tight embrace.

Major. ABHINAV SINGH

(proud, emotional)

"You did it, champ. You answered them all."

MONTAGE – THAT EVENING

The news anchors beam with excitement. Headlines flash: "Rishab Malhotra's Comeback!"

The clips of his run go viral across social media. Rishab's name trends nationwide.

RISHAB'S HOME – NIGHT

Rishab sits on the couch, bandaged but smiling. Sujatha sits beside him, holding his hand. Chethana watches the news replay — eyes glistening with pride.

Voiceover (news anchor)

"In a city of 20,000 runners, one man reminded us that the strongest muscle in the body...is the heart."

NOIDA RACE TRACK – PIT AREA

Vinod wraps up his practice laps and steps into the pit, removing his helmet. The sound of a news broadcast plays faintly from a nearby TV in the corner.

On screen: **Rishab's marathon finish** — footage of him crossing the line, collapsing, then being embraced by Major Singh.

The headline reads:

"BLADE RUNNER RISHAB MALHOTRA – A COMEBACK STORY"

Vinod turns sharply, drawn by the familiar name.

VINOD
(sarcastic, smirking)
"What's this now? Did he switch sports? Into running races these days?"

He scoffs, arms crossed.

VINOD
"And all this attention... for what? He came last, not first."

The laughter erupts from his racing crew. Loud. Mocking.

Vinod smirks, but behind the arrogance, a flicker of discomfort crosses his eye - fleeting, unspoken..

RISHAB'S BEDROOM – NIGHT

Rishab enters the room, holding the Delhi Half Marathon participation certificate in his hand.

He walks over to a shelf lined with his past glories and gently places the certificate beside his MotoGP 2 World Championship trophy.

Taking a few steps back, he stands still, eyes fixed on the display — a timeline of his journey.

Each medal, each trophy, each frame...a story of pain, perseverance and pride.

Rishab gazes in silence, not just at what he's won but at what he's reclaimed.

VIVEK'S ROOM – NIGHT

Rishab enters and finds Vivek seated at his table, focused on his studies.

RISHAB
"Hey bro...can you do me a favour?"

Vivek looks up, curious.

RISHAB
(smiling faintly)
"Can you ride me to the office tomorrow morning...on my XTR 1000?"

Vivek pauses for a moment, then nods with a warm grin.

VIVEK

"Of course. bro !!!!"

MALHOTRA'S HOME – TERRACE GARDEN - MORNING

Sujatha sits in the soft morning light, flipping through the newspaper. Her eyes stop at a headline — an article aboutRishab's incredible feat at the Delhi Half Marathon.

A smile forms on her face and her heart swells with pride.

Suddenly, a familiar roar of an engine rises from the garage below. Startled, Sujatha lowers the newspaper and hurries to the edge of the balcony. Her eyes widen.

Vivek is riding the XTR 1000 and behind him, seated confidently as pillion, is Rishab, helmet on, wind in his face.

Sujatha watches, frozen in disbelief, as her two sons ride out together and disappear into the bustling traffic beyond the gate.

MIL – BOARD ROOM

Rishab stands at the whiteboard, finishing a technical sketch. His sleeves are rolled up, energy sharp. Just then, Raj and Shekhar, both senior electrical engineers at MIL, step into the room.

RISHAB

"Thanks for coming, guys."

He gestures to the diagram on the board — a schematic of a gear shift system.

RISHAB

(determined)

"With my prosthetic leg, I can't use the traditional foot
shifter anymore. So, I've designed the gear control
mechanism to be mounted onto the handlebar — tailored
to my condition. I need your help building a custom

control unit to make this work."

Raj and Shekhar exchange puzzled glances — their boss isn't just designing. He's preparing to race.

RISHAB

(smiling, with fire in his eyes)

"I need to hit the race track again."

A beat of silence — then the two engineers nod. Determined!

MIL – BOARD ROOM – LATER

Rishab walks them through the blueprint in detail.

RISHAB

"We'll mount the gear control module on the handlebar. The high-performance sensors will send input signals to a central control unit and that unit will trigger air-pressured linear actuators to punch the gear shifts."

He pauses, letting it sink in.

RISHAB

(serious)

"It looks simple. But making all these components work in harmony — that's the real challenge."

MONTAGE – RISHAB'S WORKSHOP GRIND

After office hours, Rishab works late in the MIL garage. He meticulously fabricates parts: actuators, mounts, wiring.

Raj and Shekhar brainstorm and start building the central control unit. The blueprints are revised. Tools clank. Sparks fly. The clock is ticking and the momentum is real.

MIL GARAGE – NIGHT (AFTER A WEEK)

Raj and Shekhar unveil the completed control unit. Rishab, in parallel has the gear module and linear actuators ready.

They begin the installation and integration on the XTR 1000 — Rishab's dream machine.

TESTING PHASE

The components are in place. Rishab initiates the test. Click. Nothing. The down shift fails. Rishab frowns. He checks the sensors, then the actuators. Raj and Shekhar inspect the control unit.

SHEKHAR

"The control unit's working perfectly."

RAJ

(confirms)

"Signal flow's clean. No drop in voltage."

But the actuator still won't down shift.

MIL GARAGE – NIGHT AFTER NIGHT

Rishab stays late, hunched over the bike tracing wires, testing pressure points.

Frustration mounts. One new gear module. Same result. Failure. Again.

Time is slipping away and Rishab knows it. He sits beside the XTR 1000 in the dark garage, the only light coming from a flickering overhead lamp. His dream is within reach, but something critical stands in the way.

MIL – GARAGE – MIDNIGHT

The garage is dimly lit, silent except for the soft hum of tools and the occasional metallic clink. Rishab is deep in focus surrounded by disassembled components of the actuator kit.

He carefully tests each wire, multimeter in hand. Suddenly, he notices something — one of the sensors is overheating. He replaces it with a spare, but the problem persists.

Frustrated but methodical, Rishab removes the central control unit, tucked beside the motorcycle's battery. As he inspects the battery, his eyes narrow — it's swollen.

By digging deeper, he traces the issue back to the voltage regulator. It's faulty and sending excess voltage to the battery causing the malfunction.

Without hesitation, Rishab heads to the store room, grabs a new battery and a replacement regulator and returns to the bike. He installs both components with precision, then reassembles the actuator kit, his fingers working fast but steady.

Click. Whirr....he powers up the bike and tests the gear mechanism. The gear shifts perfectly!!

A pause...,then — Rishab jumps in pure ecstasy, letting out a triumphant breath of relief.

RISHAB

(grinning wide)

"Yes!!!"

He pulls out his phone, hands trembling with excitement, dials Salim.

The phone rings.

SALIM'S BEDROOM – NIGHT

The phone buzzes on the nightstand. Salim, groggy and half-asleep, picks it up.

SALIM

(sleepy tone)

"Bro... everything okay?"

RISHAB

(excited, breathless)

"Salim, can you come to the office right now"

SALIM

(confused)

"Now?"

RISHAB

"Yes, you heard me right — now! I need you."

MIL – GARAGE – 2:00 AM

The metal shutter creaks open as Salim rushes in, still zipping up his jacket. Rishab is already by the XTR 1000, gear parts laid out like surgical tools.

RISHAB
(excited)
"I've done it. This is the new gear-shift mechanism — designed to work without a foot lever. I want you to test it."

Salim blinks, stunned for a moment, then grins and hops onto the bike.

He rides slowly at first, cautiously feeling out the new setup. The gear shift is now controlled by a handlebar module. Rishab, meanwhile, monitors the system's feedback from his laptop — eyes darting between speed, response time and actuator pressure.

The bike picks up speed. The night echoes with the smooth hum of precision. The test continues for an hour — Salim shifting gears, cornering, braking. Rishab watches like a hawk.

SALIM
(pulling up, breathless)
"Bro, this is incredible. The response is crisp!!"

RISHAB
(proudly)
"Me and my team built it. From scratch!"

SALIM
(amazed)
"Wow..."

RISHAB
(with a knowing smile)
"I think I've hit two targets with one bullet."

Salim raises an eyebrow, puzzled.

SALIM

"And what's that ?"

RISHAB

"First — I'm going to manufacture and sell this speed shifter kit at half the price of any in the market. It'll be a first for superbikes in India. I believe this technology will give wings to many dreams."

Salim nods, impressed.

RISHAB

(eyes gleaming)

"And second — I am hitting the race track!!"

A beat, The realization hits Salim. He's speechless for a moment... then rushes forward and hugs Rishab, overcome with emotion.

MIL – TEST TRACK – MOMENTS LATER

The XTR 1000 rumbles to life.

Rishab climbs onto the bike, determination written on his face. Salim steadies it from behind. Rishab clicks the gear module with his finger — first gear engages with a sharp click.

He slowly accelerates. His hands firm, his body steady.

Both feet on the pegs. He's riding. On his own. An hour passes. Rishab finds his balance. Then... his confidence.

For the next two hours, Rishab rides under the stars, making lap after lap. Each turn sharper. Each gear shift smoother. Each corner tilt more precise.

MONTAGE – OVER THE NEXT MONTH:

Rishab practices every night after work at the Metro race academy. The XTR blurs across the track, cornering like a dream. Rishab's posture improves. His eyes grow sharper. The machine and man move as one.

Rishab is back and better than ever.

METRO RACE ACADEMY – DAY

The roar of the engine pierces the air. Rishab blazes down the track, clocking speeds of 200 kilometers per hour. His focus is razor-sharp, body aligned with the machine like a single living entity.

Bharadwaj enters the premises and stops at the edge of the track. He watches silently — observing Rishab's cornering technique, throttle control and body lean. His eyes narrow, impressed by the precision and aggression.

Rishab approaches at high speed, then slams the brakes smoothly, bringing the XTR 1000 to a perfect halt right in front of Bharadwaj.

RISHAB

(panting slightly, eyes burning with determination)
"Sir... I'm ready. Tell me..what will it take to get me to the British MotoGP?"

BHARADWAJ

(stern, calm)
"Practice. And more practice!!"

RISHAB'S INTENSE TRAINING REGIME:

Rishab's day starts at 4:00 AM sharp. A 10-kilometer run, followed by intense warm-ups and weight training until 8:00 AM. At 9:00 AM, he reports to work at MIL, grinding through his professional hours till 5:00 PM.

By 6:00 PM, he's back on the race track, pushing limits until 11:00 PM under floodlights.

Laps. Corners. Repeats.!!!

METRO RACE TRACK – NIGHT AFTER NIGHT
Rishab refines his technique under Bharadwaj's guidance. Sharper corner tilts, faster lap times and unrelenting discipline.

With every passing day, his form sharpens, his confidence returns and his name whispered in pity begins to echo in admiration once again.

Rishab is not just back... he's evolving.

RACE TRACK – PIT STOP - LATE EVENING

The sun dips below the horizon, casting a warm glow over the empty track. Rishab and Bharadwaj sit by the pit stop, huddled over a laptop, reviewing high-speed footage of Rishab's ride.

The video plays frame by frame — every lean, every turn, every millisecond matters.

They discuss riding techniques, line optimization, and braking points with laser focus.

BHARADWAJ

"Rishab, it's time we level up. You need to train on the Buddh International Circuit — and you'll do it on the latest JMC XTR 1000."

Rishab nods, absorbing the weight of the challenge.

BHARADWAJ

(firmly)

"A month of training on that track will give you a real edge. I'll get a practice slot arranged for you. In the meantime, talk to JMC and get your hands on the enhanced XTR 1000. You'll need the best machine if you're aiming for the British MotoGP."

Rishab looks out toward the darkening track, his resolve deepening.

RISHAB

"Sure, sir. I'll write to the CEO of JMC tomorrow."

That night, Rishab sits down at his desk and drafts a detailed email. He writes to Haruto Ki, the CEO of JMC, outlining his intense training regimen and his decision to compete in the World MotoGP Championship. He requests that the enhanced XTR 1000 be prepared and shipped at the earliest, emphasizing the urgency of the upcoming training phase.

JMC HEADQUARTERS, TOKYO – BOARDROOM – DAY

The sleek, glass-walled boardroom hums with quiet tension. Haruto Ki, the CEO of JMC, stands at the head of the table. Seated around him are senior directors and top executives, awaiting the agenda of this urgent meeting.

Haruto scans the room, his expression calm but purposeful.

HARUTO KI

"Good morning Gentlemen. I've called this meeting to inform you of a critical decision. JMC will participate in the World MotoGP Championship in London this year."

The room falls into stunned silence.

SENIOR DIRECTOR

(confused)

"But I thought we officially pulled out after Rishab's tragic accident. We even issued a press release about this sometime end of last year."

SECOND DIRECTOR

(leaning forward)

"Have you signed a new rider ?"

Haruto's eyes light up — not with surprise, but with conviction.

HARUTO KI

"No replacement. Rishab is returning and he will ride the XTR 1000 at the championship."

A ripple of disbelief moves across the room.

HARUTO KI

(with a proud smile)

"He sent me his recent track videos and trust me, he's not just back... he's better. I haven't seen such hunger in a rider in years."

SENIOR DIRECTOR

(Exploding with anger)

"Have you lost your mind?! You're giving our flagship superbike to a disabled man? What message does that send?"

THIRD DIRECTOR

(In disbelief)

"We'll become a global joke! Do you want JMC to be mocked for turning our engineering marvel into a charity stunt?"

Haruto stands firm, unshaken by their reactions.

HARUTO KI

(with quiet steel)

"I've already made arrangements. The practice bike will be shipped to Rishab by end of this week. I won't promise you a victory but I will promise you this: He's going to make history and JMC will be a part of it."

A beat of heavy silence.

SENIOR DIRECTOR

(coldly)

"Then mark my words, if Rishab fails to finish in the top three at the British MotoGP, I'll demand your resignation the very next day."

The directors rise, one by one and exit the boardroom without another word.

Haruto Ki remains alone at the head of the table, eyes fixed on the JMC logo on the wall. His belief in Rishab unwavering. A storm may be coming, but he stands ready.

HARUTO KI

(to himself)
"Let them doubt. I've seen fire in that man's eyes. And fire... writes legends."

MIL OFFICE – BOARDROOM – DAY

The boardroom buzzes with activity as Rishab reviews key project milestones with his technical team. Charts and schematics flash across the screen behind him.

Suddenly, an email alert pops up on his laptop. Curious, Rishab clicks it open.

His eyes widen. A smile slowly spreads across his face — a rare, heartfelt one. For a moment, the noise in the room fades into silence.

The email is from Haruto Ki, CEO of JMC.

It reads:

"We are honored by your decision to return to racing. JMC is proud to stand with you. The enhanced XTR 1000 is being built specifically for your comeback. It will reach India in two weeks. The world deserves to witness your next chapter."

Rishab leans back in his chair, his chest rising with pride and disbelief. His eyes glisten with emotion, but he holds them back.

Just then, his phone rings. The screen flashes: Coach Bharadwaj. He answers quickly.

RISHAB

"Good morning, sir."

BHARADWAJ

"Rishab, your slot at the Buddh International Circuit is booked. The training starts the moment your bike arrives."

Rishab stands up, overwhelmed, nearly speechless. His hand trembles slightly as he grips the phone tighter.

RISHAB
(voice cracking with joy)
"Sir... JMC just confirmed. The bike will be here in two weeks."

BHARADWAJ
(Pleased)
"That's fantastic. Everything's falling into place. It's your time now, Rishab."

Rishab stares out the window, eyes filled with fire and gratitude. For the first time in months, hope doesn't feel like a distant dream — it feels real!

MIL CAMPUS – DAY

Rishab, Bharadwaj and a few key members of the MIL technical team including Raj and Shekhar sit in the lounge area, eyes occasionally darting toward the campus gate.

They're waiting for something special. Something long-awaited.

The JMC XTR1000 — Rishab's machine which is scheduled for delivery today.

Suddenly, the deep rumble of a heavy engine is heard in the distance. A massive truck rolls into the MIL campus. Everyone immediately stands. Rishab's heartbeat quickens. This is it.

The truck pulls into the parking zone and comes to a halt. The air seems to still for a moment.

Two sharply dressed Japanese men step out of the vehicle and walk briskly toward the group. Rishab steps forward to greet them.

Hikaru Saito
"I am Hikaru Saito, lead engineer. This is Katashi
Nakamura, our chief mechanic from JMC."

Hands are shaken, bows exchanged, smiles polite but full of purpose.

Hikaru turns to the logistics crew and gives them a nod. With precision, the unloading begins. The container door opens and the hydraulic lifts hum. The crate is slowly lowered and wheeled into the MIL garage. The air is electric with anticipation.

Rishab and his team surround the crate. Tools come out. Screws are removed. And then the cover is pulled back. The JMC XTR 1000 stands revealed. A stunning, high-performance machine gleaming in bright yellow, like a wild beast ready to roar. Every curve speaks speed. Every inch, precision.

Rishab steps closer, mesmerized. His hand reaches out and rests gently on the tank. A moment of reverence.

RISHAB
(with emotion in his voice)
"Sir...I'm going to rock the world with this machine."

BHARADWAJ
(smiling, half-serious)
"When does the speed gear shift setup go on?"
Rishab turns toward the Japanese team, eyes focused.

RISHAB
"Gentlemen, we begin the speed shifter installation tomorrow. I hope you're ready to make magic with us."

HIKARU
(with a bow and a grin)
"It's an honor. We're excited to work alongside you."

Over the next few days, the MIL and JMC teams work in seamless coordination. Under Rishab's leadership, the speed gear shift system is successfully installed.

BUDDH INTERNATIONAL CIRCUIT – MORNING
The gates of the Buddh Circuit open to the roar of possibility. Rishab, clad in full racing gear, steps into the arena. His eyes lock onto the winding track ahead—his

battlefield.

At the pit stop, Bharadwaj stands with the crew. Salim arrives moments later, acting as Rishab's assistant during the practice sessions. He rolls out the gleaming JMC XTR 1000, positioning it at the starting grid.

BHARADWAJ
(with a proud smile)
"Welcome home, Rishab!!"

Rishab nods with a grin, walks over to the bike, and climbs aboard. He fires up the engine — **VROOOOM** — the sound echoing across the empty grandstands.

Over the following days, Rishab trains rigorously on the Buddh Circuit, pushing the limits under Bharadwaj's sharp supervision. Each lap tightens his grip on control, sharpens his reflexes and fuels his confidence. The machine and the man begin to move as one.

News of Rishab's return to the track begins to spread like wildfire. Whispers reach the offices of FMSCI.

VINOD'S HOME

Srinivasan, the Secretary of FMSCI and a close confidant of Vinod is sitting with him in the drawing room.

SRINIVASAN
"Vinod, you won't believe this — Rishab's been practicing at the Buddh Circuit. Word is he's in serious form."
Vinod's expression darkens.

BUDDH CIRCUIT – PIT STOP - EVENING

The sun dips low on the horizon as Rishab unwinds at the pit stop, sipping his protein drink after an intense session. His suit is drenched, but his spirit is calm and focused. Bharadwaj approaches him.

BHARADWAJ

"Rishab, I've scheduled a meeting with Mr. Behera tomorrow morning. 10 AM sharp. Let's meet at the FMSCI office."

RISHAB

(nodding)

"Absolutely, sir. I'll be there on time."

FMSCI HEADQUARTERS – CONFERENCE ROOM

The FMSCI President, Mr. Behera, Secretary, Srinivasan and other board members are seated in the conference room along with Rishab and Bharadwaj.

BEHERA

"So, Rishab, happy to see you bounce back after the accident. And congratulations on the Delhi Marathon achievement."

Rishab acknowledges with a nod.

BHARADWAJ

"Mr. Behera, Rishab is fully fit and ready to participate in the British MotoGP Championship."

BEHERA

(skeptical tone)

"Bharad, I know Rishab has started riding again, but that doesn't mean he's ready for international competition. This is a big stage. I hope you understand the seriousness of it."

BHARADWAJ

"Sir, I'm confident Rishab will make us proud."

BEHERA

"Even if we agree, will the international body allow a handicapped rider to compete?"

BHARADWAJ

"Sir, Oscar Pistorius was allowed to compete in the London 2012 Olympics after his appeal was accepted by the Court of Arbitration for Sport."

SRINIVASAN

(sarcastic tone)

"Just because you ran a half marathon doesn't mean you're licensed to race in MotoGP. This is MotoGP, for God's sake. Do you understand?"

Rishab sits silently, listening.

BEHERA

(looking at Rishab)

"Rishab, we've already announced India's official entry."

RISHAB

(sternly)

"I'm still the Moto2 Champion and a legally qualified participant for the World MotoGP Championship."

Behera after a deep thought.

BEHERA

"Give us some time. Can you both please wait at the reception?"

Rishab and Bharadwaj exit and wait at the reception.

15 MINUTES LATER:

Behera and the other board members approach the two men.

BEHERA

"We're sorry, Rishab. The board does not have confidence in your participation. This is a world stage, and we can't risk the reputation of our country."

Behera and his group walk away, laughing and mocking Rishab's situation.

Rishab, determined, decides to meet the Sports Minister. He visits the Ministry several times before finally securing an appointment.

❧❧❧

MINISTRY OF YOUTH AFFAIRS AND SPORTS – DAY

Rishab waits patiently at the reception, eyes steady, nerves hidden beneath calm determination. The secretary approaches.

SECRETARY

"Mr. Rishab, the Minister will see you now."

The secretary escorts him down the corridor and opens the door to the Minister's cabin.

Inside, Vikas Jain, the Sports Minister rises from his chair with a warm smile. He walks toward Rishab and embraces him.

VIKAS JAIN

"Rishab! I'm so proud of you. You've become an inspiration to millions."

RISHAB

"Thank you, sir. I'm honored to be here."

As Rishab steps further in, his smile fades — seated inside are Behera, Vinod, and Srinivasan watching him silently.

VIKAS JAIN

"How have things been at your end?"

RISHAB

"Sir, I want to compete in the British MotoGP Championship and I'm here to ask for your support to make that possible."

The Minister's smile drops. The room falls into a tense silence.

VIKAS JAIN

(stern)

"Are you serious, young man? You think you can race with your condition?"

Without hesitation, Rishab unzips his bag and pulls out a folder and a pen drive, placing them firmly on the desk.

RISHAB

"These are my medical fitness reports and video footage of my practice sessions. Every second on that track proves I'm ready."

VIKAS JAIN

"I'm not an expert on the technicalities of racing. I'll have to rely on the FMSCI. If they clear you, I have no objection."

BEHERA

"Mr. Minister, with all due respect, this is unprecedented. No physically challenged rider has ever competed at this level. We cannot allow it."

VIKAS JAIN

(frustrated)

"If the governing body doesn't authorize you, Rishab, my hands are tied."

Rishab stands, quietly gathering his documents and pen drive.

RISHAB

(disappointed, steady)

"I truly believed I'd find support here. It's unfortunate that even your hands are bound. My only option now is to appeal to the Court of Arbitration for Sport."

Suddenly, Vinod leaps from his chair, furious. He strides toward Rishab and shoves him violently to the floor.

VINOD

(shouting)

"This race is mine, Rishab! You're not stealing it from me!"

Rishab crashes down. Shock. Silence. Then chaos. Vikas Jain and Behera rush to Rishab's side, helping him up

VIKAS JAIN

(boiling with anger)

"Vinod, get out NOW!!. I don't want you in my office."

Vinod glares, but backs off. He and Srinivasan storm out, slamming the door behind them. Rishab steadies himself, brushes the dust off his clothes and walks out, dignified but wounded.

The Minister watches him go, then turns to Behera.

VIKAS JAIN

(coldly)

"Behera, I want your organization to assess Rishab. Test him, verify his fitness and give me an official report. I will not have this turn into a scandal. We have elections in five states in the next two months and I don't want any controversies at this stage."

BEHERA

"Don't worry, sir. I'll take care of it."

VIKAS JAIN

(sternly)

"You'd better."

Behera nods and quietly exits the chamber.

FMSCI HEADQUARTERS – DAY

The air in the conference room is thick with tension. The entire board of FMSCI officials is present. At the canter sits Mr. Behera, eyes sharp and calculating. Rishab and Bharadwaj are seated across from him.

MR. BEHERA

(looking directly at Rishab)

"Well...since you insist on racing, we need to be sure you're truly ready. We're not just testing your fitness, we're testing whether you still carry the fire of a champion."

RISHAB
(without hesitation)
"I'm ready. Run your test."

BEHERA
(leaning forward)
"Very well. If you can beat your own Moto2 lap record, you'll have our approval. Two laps. Four minutes. No excuses."

BHARADWAJ
(shocked, almost yelling)
"What?! Sir, that's insane! His record time was 5.7 minutes!"

BEHERA
(calmly, coldly)
"That was on a 500cc. This time, you'll be on a 1000cc machine. The stakes are higher. So is the speed."

RISHAB
(locked in, eyes blazing)
"I'm game."

BEHERA
(with finality)
"Then we'll see you on Sunday at the track."

Bharadwaj, frustrated, slams his fist on the table. The sound echoes in the room. Behera doesn't flinch, but Rishab remains calm, focused. His resolve unshaken.

Rishab's eyes meet Behera's —no fear, only fire.

KARUNYA – EVENING

Rishab and Chethana sit quietly in the garden area. The golden hue of the setting sun casts a warm glow around them. A soft breeze stirs the leaves as tension and excitement linger in the air.

RISHAB
(Taking a deep breath)
"Tomorrow's a big day for me...I have to prove that I'm worthy — not just to them, but to myself."

CHETHANA
(Gently, with unwavering confidence)
"You will win this, Rishab. I believe in you."

RISHAB
(Looking at her, hopeful)
"Will you be there tomorrow morning? At the Buddh Circuit?"

CHETHANA
(Smiling warmly, taking his hand)
"Of course, Champ. I wouldn't miss it for the world."

That same evening at the Buddh International Circuit, the powerful JMC XTR 1000 roars into the paddock before falling silent. It's wheeled carefully into the PIT number 10, the sound of footsteps echoing under the metallic roof. The night shift guard steps in, does a final check, then locks the garage door with a loud click sealing the machine in silence, ready for battle.

BUDDH RACE TRACK – MORNING, 9:00 AM

The grandstands shimmer under the morning sun. The VIP Lounge, perched beside the starting point, hosts the stern faces of the FMSCI board members. Among them, Behera sits, arms crossed, watching silently.

At the pit stop, a palpable tension fills the air. Chethana, Bharadwaj along with Salim and the technical crew stand waiting, eyes darting between the track and the paddock entrance.

Suddenly, the roar of tire treads scraping the asphalt cuts through the silence. Katashi Nakamura, the chief mechanic, hauls the gleaming JMC XTR 1000 to the track and positions it behind the start line.

Moments later, Rishab steps out from the dressing room, clad in full racing gear — a symbol of grit, passion, and defiance. His eyes are fierce, yet calm. The elite crowd begins to murmur as the stage is now truly set.

A massive LED display lights up with the target time. The challenge is on.

Rishab walks toward the bike like a warrior to his battlefield. He mounts it, closes his eyes, and draws a deep breath. The engine ignites with a thunderous roar — a beast awakened. He takes off for a warm-up lap, tearing through the track like lightning.

He returns to the start line, revving the engine, eyes locked forward. The technical crew hits record. Everyone holds their breath.

The hooter blows. And he's off.

MONTAGE – RISHAB'S RACE

Rishab accelerates like a bullet, his movements seamless and precise. He carves through the corners with surgical accuracy, the JMC XTR roaring under his command.

LAP 1 — completed in under two minutes. A new record !!

Chethana's heart races. Her hands tremble. Her eyes refuse to blink.

Rishab enters LAP 2, faster, sharper, braver. His timing is flawless. Even the board members begin to lean forward, their skepticism turning into stunned admiration.

The LED board ticks mercilessly. Rishab hurtles towards the final stretch.

Then — the unthinkable.

As Rishab leans into the final left corner, the rear tire twitches — a split second betrayal. The motorcycle skids violently. Rishab is thrown off. His prosthetic leg detaches mid-air, spiraling as his body crashes and skids along the tarmac. The JMC XTR flips — once, twice — then slams into the barricade, erupting into a shower of debris.

SILENCE. THEN CHAOS.

Chethana screams. Bharadwaj, Salim and the crew sprint. The board members rise in shock. People are yelling. Cameras flash. Whispers turn into roars.

Chethana reaches Rishab first, drops to her knees, and lifts his head onto her lap. Her hands fumble desperately with his helmet.

CHETHANA

(tears streaming, panicked)

"Rishab! Rishab, can you hear me? Open your eyes, please!"

She taps his cheeks, voice cracking. Finally, she removes the helmet. His face is bloodied, eyes fluttering. He looks at her, in agony but conscious.

RISHAB

(breathing heavily)

"The... handle... fork..."

Hearing Rishab, Katashi bolts toward the wreck. He examines the handlebars, picks up the bike and tries pushing, but it won't steer straight.

KATASHI

(suspiciously)

"Something's not right..."

He signals to the crew. They stabilize the bike and begin diagnostics on the spot.

AMBULANCE BAY – MOMENTS LATER

Chethana,Salim and the doctor are in the ambulance with Rishab. As Bharadwaj tries to board, Katashi grabs by the arm.

KATASHI

(grave tone)

"Bharadwaj...wait. Someone tampered with the fork settings."

Stunned, Bharadwaj steps back. The ambulance doors shut. It speeds away, sirens screaming.

PIT AREA:

BHARADWAJ

(tense)

"Are you sure?"

Katashi nods as a crew member brings over a laptop.

KATASHI

(looking at data)

"Just as I feared — massive deviation in the steering geometry. The front fork preload is off. The rear shocks too hard. Compression stroke ruined. That corner was impossible to take cleanly."

BHARADWAJ

(checking the logs)

"Was everything fine when the bike left MIL campus?"

KATASHI

"I have the data from last night. It was perfect then."

Bharadwaj's expression darkens. He storms toward security.

BHARADWAJ

"Who was on duty last night at PIT 10?"

SECURITY

"Ram Singh, sir."

BHARADWAJ

"Call him. Now."

SECURITY BAY:

The call connects. Bharadwaj grabs the phone.

BHARADWAJ

(intense)

"Ram Singh? It's Bharad. Who accessed PIT 10 last night?"

RAM SINGH

(voice trembling)

"S-Sir... what happened?"

BHARADWAJ

(furious)

"Answer the damn question! WHO was there?"

Silence.....

Bharadwaj turns slowly — his eyes lock onto Srinivasan, standing behind Behera, visibly shaken.

BHARADWAJ

(through gritted teeth, still on phone)

"It was Srinivasan...wasn't it?"

Hearing this, Srinivasan bolts. Bharadwaj drops the phone and gives a chase — tackles him hard to the ground. He grabs the helmet from the track and raises it in fury. He's about to smash it on Srinivasan.

BEHERA

(shouting)

"STOP IT, BHARADWAJ! LEAVE HIM!"

Bharadwaj freezes, chest heaving. Slowly, he lowers the helmet... and smashes it onto the ground instead. It shatters.

He walks away, each step heavier than the last, eyes brimming with tears, rage burning beneath the surface.

Behind him, Behera stands still on the track, surrounded by silence and shattered trust....

MALHOTRA HOME – LATE EVENING.

The doorbell rings sharply. Sujatha walks to the door, wiping her hands nervously on her dupatta. She opens it to find Chethana standing outside, pale and shaken.

CHETHANA

(trembling, eyes filled with fear)
"Maa... please... can you come with me?"
SUJATHA
(concerned, voice cracking)
"What happened? Is everything alright?"
CHETHANA
(softly)
"Please... just come."
CITY SPECIALITY HOSPITAL – RISHAB'S WARD

Inside the sterile ward, Rishab lies on the hospital bed, bandaged and bruised. The doctor examines him as Bharadwaj and Salim stand nearby, silent and tense.

The door creaks open. Sujatha enters with Chethana. She stops in her tracks, her eyes locking on her son. Her face crumbles. She rushes to his side, tears rolling down her cheeks.

SUJATHA
(whispers)
"Rishab..."
The doctor turns to her with a calm demeanor.
DOCTOR
"Ma'am, please don't worry. He's stable. He's sprained his wrist and injured his stump, but it's nothing critical. We'll keep him overnight for observation. He can go home tomorrow evening... and, with care, he'll be back on the track in a week."
Sujatha folds her hands gratefully.
SUJATHA
"Thank you, doctor."
The doctor gives Rishab a reassuring nod and exits. A silence falls. Sujatha's expression hardens as she turns to the others.
SUJATHA

(sternly)

"I need to speak to my son. Give us some privacy now, please."

Without a word Bharadwaj, Salim, and Chethana exit the ward. The door closes behind them.

HOSPITAL WARD – CONTINUOUS

Sujatha sits beside Rishab. She takes his hand, her voice trembling.

SUJATHA

(soft but firm)

"You've started riding again...?"

RISHAB

(softly)

"Maa, I'm fine. It wasn't a mistake...there was a technical fault. That's why it happened."

SUJATHA

(a flicker of panic)

"A technical fault? And what if there's another one? What if next time you don't get up?"

RISHAB

"Maa, please...you know this isn't just my dream. It was Papa's too."

Sujatha looks into his eyes — a mirror of his father's. That same fire. That same madness. Her lips quiver.

SUJATHA

"So it's decided. You're going to race?"

RISHAB

"Yes, Maa. I have no choice..."

She looks away, broken. The strength she's carried all these months shatters. She leans into his shoulder and weeps — not just in fear, but in helplessness. The son she tried to protect from danger is running toward it, with purpose.

HOSPITAL CORRIDOR – MOMENTS LATER

Sujatha storms out, her steps staggered. Chethana follows her, worried.

MALHOTRA HOME – NIGHT

Sujatha bursts into the living room. She walks up to Vijay's portrait, staring into his smile frozen in time. Her shoulders tremble. Then she collapses to her knees, crying uncontrollably.

SUJATHA

(voice breaking)

"He's just like you...stubborn, fearless and I don't know how to stop him."

Chethana kneels beside her, gently embracing her from behind. Her voice is soft, steady, but full of emotion.

CHETHANA

"Maa... Rishab's heart beats on the track. He's walking the path his father once dreamed for him. And now, more than ever...he needs you — your faith, your strength, your love."

Sujatha slowly turns and embraces Chethana tightly. The two women hold onto each other — one as a grieving mother, the other as a steadfast supporter. The quiet of the room is heavy with pain, but also a growing sense of resolve.

CHAPTER FIVE

ASCENSION

HOSPITAL WARD – DAY

Rishab lies in bed, his heart bruised but burning with quiet determination. Bharadwaj stands by the window, fists clenched. Salim paces nervously.

SALIM

(anxious, voice cracking)

"What now, bro? After all this... will they ever let you race again?"

BHARADWAJ

(furious)

"To hell with them. Let's drag those bastards to court. The association members, the minister — every last one of them."

Rishab turns his head slowly, his voice soft but steady —dangerously calm.

RISHAB

(low, intense)

"I will go to the court but to people's court. Let them decide now!"

Bharadwaj and Salim exchange confused glances.

BHARADWAJ

(startled)

"What are you talking about?"

RISHAB

(eyes gleaming)

"I have a plan. But I can't do it alone. Will you both stand with me?"

A beat of silence. Then, without a word, Bharadwaj and Salim step closer. The three men lean in as Rishab, voice low, begins to explain the plan. Their eyes burn with shared purpose.

HOSPITAL – EVENING – RECEPTION AREA

Rishab is wheeled out of the ward by Bharadwaj, his injuries more visible now — forehead bandaged, arm in a sling, leg heavily wrapped. His posture may be broken, but his eyes blaze with fire.

As they turn the corner into the lobby, the air is electric.

A crowd of nearly 100 people is gathered outside the hospital gates, chanting fiercely:

CROWD

"Justice for Rishab!"

"Down with FMSCI!"

"Let him race!"

Salim leads the protest from the front, megaphone in hand, voice booming.

Protesters wave placards, some with Rishab's face, others with slogans condemning corruption in motorsport.

Half a dozen reporters are already on the scene, microphones ready, cameras rolling. Several others wait anxiously to catch a glimpse of Rishab.

The POLICE arrive and begin setting up barricades to manage the growing tension.

Bharadwaj, fire in his eyes, steps forward holding a bunch of pen drives. He walks straight to the media pack, voice raised above the chaos.

BHARADWAJ

(raging)

"Look at him! This—this—is your national champion! Qualified to represent India at the MotoGP World Championship. And what did they do? They sabotaged his bike. They threw him off the track. Now he's in a wheelchair, not because of an accident, but because of a conspiracy."

Gasps ripple through the reporters. The cameras zoom in on Rishab.

BHARADWAJ

(holds up the pen drives)

"Here. Footage of every test session. See for yourself — his form, his speed, his record-breaking LAP 1. He was ready. He IS ready."

Bharadwaj begins handing out the pen drives as reporters scramble for copies. News vans broadcast live. The social media too explodes.

MONTAGE – NEWS COVERAGE & SOCIAL MEDIA

#RishabForMotoGP trends globally within hours. Clips of his LAP 1 record spread like wildfire.

TV anchors shout over each other in prime-time debates. The FMSCI officials dodge uncomfortable questions. The Sports Minister's office issues a vague statement. Fans and motorsport enthusiasts from across the world tweet in support.

INTERNATIONAL HEADLINE:

"India's MotoGP Hero Sabotaged? Outrage Erupts Over Rishab Malhotra's Crash"

ON TV – EXPERT PANEL

"If this is true, then someone tried to end his career before it even began. And yet, the world is now watching and waiting."

@FIM HEADQUARTERS:

A group of FIM EXECUTIVES sit in a dark room watching Rishab's test footage. His speed, agility, and control speak louder than any words. One executive leans forward, impressed.

FIM EXECUTIVE
(gravely)
"He belongs on that grid."

@FMSCI HEADQUARTERS

The sterile silence of the office is shattered by the shrill ring of Behera's phone. He checks the caller ID — his face tightens. It's the Sports Minister. He answers, and before he can speak—

VIKAS JAIN
(furious, roaring)
"What the hell is going on, Behera?! I warned you, didn't I? And yet, you've let this explode in our faces!"

BEHERA
(stammering)
"I-I know, sir. Things spun out of control. I've already fired Srinivasan."

VIKAS JAIN
(snarling)
"Firing that idiot won't clean up the mess! The media is eating us alive. There's public outrage, international pressure... We're getting slaughtered. What's your plan to fix this?"

A long pause. Behera takes a deep breath.

BEHERA
(flat but resolute)
"We let Rishab race."

A beat of silence on the other end.

VIKAS JAIN

(coldly)

"Can he even do it?"

BEHERA

(firm)

"I've seen him ride. He's in phenomenal form. He nearly beat Alessandro's time in the test lap.

If anyone can make a mark for India, it's him."

A heavy sigh from the other end.

VIKAS JAIN

"Fine. I've got a live interview tonight. I'll make the announcement myself.

You get everything ready. Paperwork, clearances, travel — I want Rishab on that flight to London."

BEHERA

"Yes, sir."

The call ends. Behera slumps back in his chair, rubbing his temples — the weight of politics, scandal, and redemption pressing down on him.

NEWSROOM – LATE EVENING

Bright lights, cameras rolling. The Sports Minister, Vikas Jain, sits across from a primetime anchor. The nation watches in suspense.

VIKAS JAIN

(earnest, but polished)

"The government has moved mountains to ensure Rishab Malhotra competes in the MotoGP World Championship.

We've made difficult decisions and overcome intense pressure — all to protect the spirit of Indian motorsport.

Rishab is not just a racer — he's a symbol of courage, resilience and national pride."

RISHAB'S BEDROOM – NIGHT

Rishab lies on his bed, watching the announcement on TV. As the words sink in, a faint smile touches his lips — not of pride, but quiet vindication.

He rises slowly, walks over to his father's portrait on the wall. He stands in silence, eyes locked with his father's image, voice barely a whisper.

RISHAB
(softly)
"We're going to London, Papa.."

VINOD'S HOME – NIGHT

Vinod stands in front of his TV, eyes wide with disbelief. The minister's words echo in the room. His face twists with rage. He snatches his phone and dials furiously. The call connects.

VINOD
(seething)
"Behera... are you serious? Now a disabled man is going to represent India on the world stage?"

BEHERA
(resigned)
"My hands are tied, Vinod. The decision's been made."

VINOD
(roaring)
"To hell with your decisions! And to hell with you!"

He slams the phone down so hard it cracks. His breathing is erratic. He storms across the room, knocking a glass off the table. It shatters. Vinod's rage burns unchecked — fueled not just by prejudice, but by fear of being overshadowed by the very man he tried to erase.

After a week's rest, Rishab and the team prepare for their boot camp at the Madras Race Academy.

As the JMC racing team gears up for the final boot camp, no companies come forward to sponsor Rishab except for his own company MIL and his partner JMC.

The FMSCI also fails to provide an International coach as nobody wants to put their coaching career on the line for Rishab.

BUDDH CIRCUIT – NIGHT – PIT STOP

The hum of engines dies down. Under the glowing floodlights, Rishab finishes his final practice lap. Sweat drips from his face. Bharadwaj stands at the edge of the track, reviewing telemetry, scribbling notes with intensity.

RISHAB

(catching his breath)

"Sir...so it's true? No international coach wants to train me?"

BHARADWAJ

(sighs, frustrated)

"That's the case, Rishab. This is the MotoGP World championship. You're up against the best and coaching you for the battle... it's seen as a risk. A career-ending one."

Rishab looks away for a moment, then turns back, defiant.

RISHAB

(sincerely)

"I don't care about them. Will you coach me at the MRA?"

BHARADWAJ

(hesitating)

"Rishab... I've trained riders, yes — but never for this. I'm not sure I have what it takes to get you there..."

RISHAB

(stepping closer)

"I have confidence in you, sir. That's all I need."

A long pause. Then, Bharadwaj places a hand on Rishab's shoulder and pulls him into a tight embrace.

RISHAB

(whispers)

"I just hope I'm not putting your career on the line..."

BHARADWAJ

(emotional)

"Damn my career. I just want to see you conquer the Silverstone park."

MONTAGE – TRAINING AT MADRAS RACE ACADEMY

Rishab, Bharadwaj and the racing team fly to Chennai. The boot camp begins — and it's brutal.

16 hours of track time every single day. Sweat. Pain. Progress.

Bharadwaj throws everything he has at Rishab — race lines, braking techniques, body positioning, throttle control, exit strategy and frame-by-frame breakdowns of the Silverstone Circuit.

They study every bump, every curve, every corner. But an issue keeps resurfacing — **THE LEFT CORNER.**

Every time Rishab approaches a sharp left, there's hesitation. A mental block. A ghost from the crash at Buddh Circuit that still lingers. He can't shake the fear of falling. And it's costing him time.

@MRA TRACKSIDE – NIGHT

Under a dim lamp, Rishab and Bharadwaj study slow-motion race replays. Notes fill the whiteboard. Diagrams of Silverstone's layout cover the walls. They watch Alessandro's riding style, frame by frame.

Bharadwaj even pores through championship articles late into the night, extracting insights from legends and old pros. Every tiny advantage is noted, discussed, tested.

But despite all progress — two major concerns remain.

MRA – PIT STOP – EVENING

Rishab sits at the monitor, watching his latest lap time. It's good — but not great. Bharadwaj walks in, holding a cup of coffee. He places it beside Rishab.

BHARADWAJ

(somber)

"So... we're at the end of the boot camp. You've grown faster, sharper — no doubt. But two issues still haunt us."

RISHAB

(quietly)

"The start... and the left corners."

BHARADWAJ

(nods)

"You take too long to plant your left foot on the peg when launching from the grid. It's costing you the acceleration burst. And that corner phobia... it's still in your head, Rishab. If you can beat that fear and trust yourself again — you can go toe to toe with Alessandro."

A long silence. Rishab doesn't respond. Instead, he looks down at his prosthetic leg. A man facing not just the competition — but himself.

KARUNYA – MORNING

The sun filters softly through the old windows of Karunya. The air is filled with warmth and a sense of departure.

Rishab sits at the long breakfast table, sharing a quiet meal with the inmates of the old age home. Laughter is light, but hearts are heavy. For them, he's more than a racer — he's a symbol of hope.

@ The Garden.

Cpt. Chatterjee, Salim, and Chethana standing under an old tree along with Rishab.

Cpt. CHATTERJEE
(emotional, proud)

"Son... I'm so proud of you. You'll have all our blessings.

Every prayer we utter will carry your name."

Rishab bends down and touches Mr. Chatterjee's feet. The old man gently places his hand on Rishab's head, eyes misty with emotion.

Rishab turns to Salim. The hug they share is tight, brotherly, and filled with unspoken gratitude.

Then he faces Chethana. Their eyes lock. No words come. They don't need to. In that gaze, there's a storm of emotion — love, fear, hope, and everything in between.

Rishab takes a step closer. He wants to embrace her, to tell her everything he's holding inside... but something holds him back. So he stops. She stands still, her hands clenched, her heart racing — but her lips stay sealed.

Just then, Rocket runs toward Rishab barking joyfully. Rishab kneels, burying his hand in Rocket's fur, holding back tears.

He rises and begins walking to his car. And then—

CHETHANA
(calling out, voice trembling)

"Rishab...!"

He stops. Turns. She walks up to him slowly, her eyes shining.

CHETHANA
(softly)

"Take care of yourself."

RISHAB

(smiling faintly)
"I'll miss you at Silverstone."
CHETHANA
(with emotion)
"I'm always with you...All the best, Champ."
Rishab gazes at her one last time, then nods and walks away, his footsteps heavy with unsaid goodbyes.

MALHOTRA HOME – BALCONY
The evening sky is painted in hues of fire and ash. Rishab enters the balcony and finds his mother, Sujatha, asleep on the sofa. A copy of the Bhagavad Gita rests on her lap.

He kneels beside her quietly, then lays his head on her lap. She stirs, opens her eyes slowly and places a trembling hand on his hair.

RISHAB
(soft, resolute)
"Maa...I want the world to know — I'm not physically challenged. I'm a challenger. This race... it's no longer just mine. It's for everyone who's ever been doubted, for every soul that's been told they can't. My victory will be their victory."
Sujatha, unable to speak, leans forward and plants a gentle kiss on his forehead. Her eyes glisten as she cradles her son — the warrior she's raised.

The moment is sacred. A quiet promise is made beneath the stars.

SILVERSTONE CIRCUIT – ENGLAND

Three gleaming JMC XTR 1000 bikes arrive at the track. The pit lane is alive with the energy of a world championship.

The technicians swiftly set up the speed gear shifter system on the three XTR 1000 motorcycles. The engines are tested. The tyre pressure, suspension, telemetry, every detail is tuned to perfection.

The machines are ready. Now, all eyes are on the man who rides them.

SILVERSTONE CIRCUIT – DAY

The sun glints off the tarmac of the legendary Silverstone track. It's Saturday — Free Practice Day.

Three intense 45-minute sessions lie ahead. The combined times from these sessions will determine who qualifies directly for Sunday's main event...and who must battle again in the dreaded qualifier.

A convoy of trailers and team trucks lines the paddock. The JMC XTR Team van pulls in. Rishab, lean, focused, and wide-eyed with adrenaline, steps out and breathes in the moment.

He walks onto the track. Around him, 20 elite teams prepare for war. Engines hum. Mechanics work with military precision. It's part meet-and-greet, part silent prelude to chaos.

Suddenly, cutting through the crowd like royalty — Alessandro, the reigning MotoGP World Champion, strides toward Rishab.

ALESSANDRO

(offering a hand)

"All the best, mate."

RISHAB

(eyes lighting up, voice trembling with excitement)

"Thank you, Alessandro. It's... it's an honor. You're an

inspiration."
ALESSANDRO
"Ride well."
RISHAB
"I will. Thank you."

Alessandro nods, but doesn't walk away just yet. He's been watching Rishab's rise. He knows the kid's got fire, but also that fire alone won't be enough.

The course run concludes. Engines start to growl. Thefirst free practice session is moments away.

The JMC XTR crew swarms Rishab's bike for a final check.

The racers line up. **The hooter blares.**

A thunderous roar erupts. The pack launches forward.

Except — Rishab stumbles.

His left foot lags, missing the peg by a split-second. That half-second hesitation kills his acceleration off the line.

Midway through the session, Rishab claws back — dancing through straight lines with grace, attacking right corners with precision. But the left turns... they haunt him. He slows, unsure, shaving crucial seconds off his time.

Every missed apex. Every moment of hesitation. It costs him.

JMC XTR PIT – POST SESSION

Bharadwaj, looks at the timing sheet. His face hardens. Rishab places 16th.

BHARADWAJ
(quietly, to his crew)
"This won't cut it."

MONTAGE – SECOND & THIRD PRACTICE SESSIONS:

Rishab launching better, but still slightly late. The right corners are fast, clean and surgical, but left corners still faltering, again in straightaways he is flying. He fights. He adapts. But he never breaks through.

As the third session ends, the final times are tallied. Tension coils around the paddock like smoke.

The top 10 will race on Sunday. The rest will have to give one more shot in the qualifier.

CIRCUIT – TIMING BOARD – MOMENTS LATER

Beep. Beep. Beep. The board flashes the final standings.

RISHAB — Is placed at **Position 15**.

Gasps. Groans. And silence. He didn't make it. He will have to fight again — in the brutal, do-or-die qualifier. Only two spots remain.

@ JMC XTR PIT – DUSK

Rishab storms into the pit. He rips off his gloves, throws down his helmet. His breath is shallow. Rage mixes with despair.

RISHAB

(to himself)

"If I can't fix the start... If I can't take those lefts..."

He stops. Words fail. He unzips his duffel and reaches in slowly pulling out a worn photograph.

His father — smiling, proud, holding a younger Rishab by the shoulders. Rishab stares. Tears fall silently.

The low hum of the pit fades beneath the weight of silence. Rishab sits alone, clutching the photograph of his father.

RISHAB

(softly, trembling)

"Papa...I'm sorry. I've let you down. I've let my country down."

He stares at the photo, his jaw clenched, eyes glistening. Suddenly—

ANNOUNCER

"Riders for the Qualifier, please proceed to the grid."
"Repeat: Riders to the grid."

Rishab blinks. Focus returns to his eyes like a spark reigniting. He places the photo gently back into his bag and rises.

CLICK !! He feels something shift in his left leg — a faint but sharp click. His eyes widen. A realization.

PUB – Somewhere in the countryside of Italy:

A crowded pub buzzes with energy. Loud music, laughter, glasses clinking.

At one corner, a massive TV draws a crowd. The MotoGP Qualifier is airing live. The atmosphere is electric. Betting slips fly. Cheers rise.

Flavio, the pub's charismatic, sharp-eyed owner, watches like a hawk as fans throw down cash on Alessandro and Martin Marique, the world no. 2.

FLAVIO

"Come on, boys. Let's see some speed. This is where the real money rides."

He pockets a wad of notes with a smirk.

Stephano, a weathered farmer in dusty clothes, enters. He orders a beer and quietly settles near the screen. His eyes flicker across the room — everyone betting on European giants.

But on screen, something unexpected is happening.

SILVERSTONE CIRCUIT – STARTING GRID

The nine riders wheel their machines into place. Engines idle like growling beasts waiting to be unleashed.

Suddenly, heads turn. Rishabemerges from the tunnel, walking with determination past the pit wall.

Gasps ripple through the pit crew. Even Bharadwaj is frozen in shock.

Rishab's racing suit has been cut — clean above the left knee. His prosthetic leg gleams under the floodlights.

He didn't make an excuse. He made an adjustment. The tight racing suit had restricted the suction seal of his prosthetic knee. It delayed his takeoff. But now, with the suit cut, the joint moves freely.

The cameras zoom in. The world sees it. The crowd falls into stunned silence.

COMMENTATOR

"That's... Rishab. And he's exposing his prosthetic leg. This...this is unprecedented."

Racers exchange looks. Some in awe. Some in disbelief.

Rishab doesn't flinch. He grabs his bike. With help from his team, he rolls it to the grid. He mounts the machine. The visor comes down.

COMMENTATOR

"Ladies and gentlemen...history is being written tonight."

@ FLAVIO'S PUB

The pub is loud and rowdy — a storm of laughter, beer and betting. But as the live broadcast flickers on the screen, a collective silence falls.

Rishab is on-screen, stepping toward his bike — hisprosthetic leg exposed.

A stunned murmur rolls through the room.

FLAVIO

"Is that—? Is that the one-legged racer?"

Gasps. Disbelief. Someone bursts out—

GAMBLER

"The one-legged racer?! This has to be a joke!"

Stephano, sitting quietly in the corner with his beer, leans forward. His eyes narrow. He walks toward the TV, almost pulled in by the image of Rishab.

GAMBLER
(shouting)
"Hey! Idiot! Move away from the screen — you're blocking the view!"

Laughter erupts behind him.

FLAVIO
(mocking, loud enough for everyone to hear)
"Any brave soul here stupid enough to bet on the half-legged racer?"

More laughter, louder this time. Flavio basks in it.

STEPHANO
(firm, cutting through the noise)
"I will."

The laughter fades.

He walks up to Flavio's table. Slowly, defiantly, he reaches into his worn-out pockets and pulls out a handful of coins and small notes. He places them on the table.

STEPHANO (CONT'D)
"That's all I've got. It's enough for me."

Before Flavio can react, one of his bouncers shoves Stephano hard.

BOUNCER
"Are you out of your damn mind? Can you even pay for your beer? Drink it and get out!"

Stephano crashes to the floor. The pub erupts again — this time in cruel, humiliating laughter.

He says nothing. No protest. He gets up slowly, his jaw clenched, his pride shattered and walks out into the cold night.

STEPHANO'S HOUSE

The door swings open violently.

BEDROOM – CONTINUOUS

Stephano enters, the beer bottle still in his hand. His eyes land on MARIO, his teenage son, sleeping in bed — frail, pale, lost in his own world.

Stephano walks to him and gently places a hand on his forehead. Tears fill his eyes.

CUT TO FLASHBACK:

A CITY IN ITALY – AT THE TRAFFIC SIGNAL – DAY

Mario, full of life, pedals his bicycle toward college. He stops at a red signal. From behind — a truck barrels forward, brakes screeching too late— **CRASH.**

Blood. Screams. Silence.

CUT TO PRESENT:

@ MARIO'S BEDROOM

Stephano's face is stone. His son lost both legs. Lost his future and Stephano lost everything trying to save him.

@ DRAWING ROOM

Stephano rushes to the cupboard, rips open drawers — finds a few crumpled notes. He heads to the bookshelf, lifts an old book — finds coins tucked inside. He gathers everything. Every last cent.

SILVERSTONE CIRCUIT – THE QUALIFIER

The hooter blares. Tires screech.

Rishab launches — this time with perfect takeoff. His left leg hits the peg in sync, fluid and fast.

Bharadwaj and the JMC crew erupt in cheers.

TRACK – LAP 5

Rishab's bike starts to falter — engine sputtering. He senses it immediately. Without panic, he veers into the pit lane. The JMC crew is ready. The new bike is already prepped. In a single motion, Rishab leaps off the old and onto the new.

ZOOM. He's gone.

RACE MONTAGE

Rishab leans into the throttle, the engine screaming beneath him like a beast unleashed. He slices through the track like a scalpel — smooth, fearless, razor-sharp.

He nails every right corner. His body leans with bullet-like precision, knees grazing the tarmac, balance locked in. On the straight lanes, he's a missile — the speedometer climbing, blurring everything around him. One rider down. Another overtaken. He's hunting them — one by one — with unrelenting precision. Sweat drips down his temple. His jaw clenched. The world narrows to throttle, grip, breath.

SILVERSTONE CIRCUIT – FINAL LAP

The crowd is on their feet. The commentators are screaming.

COMMENTATOR

"He's gaining! Rishab is gaining on the leaders!"

Ahead — two bikes. He picks his line. Eyes sharp. Everything slows.

He dives into the final right turn — commits everything — tires biting the asphalt, bike trembling on the edge of control.

Exit clean. Full throttle. Final stretch.

He closes in, One down. Now neck and neck for second place. With a final surge — he edges forward. Front wheel crosses. Checkered flag waves.

QUALIFIER RACE RESULT FLASHES ON SCREEN

Rishab is placed in 2nd position and qualifies for the BIG RACE !!

The JMC PIT CREW ERUPTS.Fists pump. Mechanics scream. Bharadwaj leaps over the barrier.

BHARADWAJ

"HE'S IN! HE'S IN!!"

Rishab, exhausted, exhales hard as the bike rolls to a stop. He looks up, chest rising and falling — a storm of emotion behind the visor.

He did it, not just for the race but for hisfather, his country and for himself !!!

CHEERS explode in the JMC pit. Bharadwaj sprints to the track, throws his arms around Rishab.

@ ALESSANDRO'S PIT

Alessandro and his team watch silently.

COACH

"He's fixed one piece of the puzzle... Let's see what he does tomorrow."

ALESSANDRO

(smiling faintly)

"Tomorrow... will be very interesting."

@ FLAVIO'S PUB – NIGHT

The entire pub is dead silent. No cheers. No laughter. Just shock. The TV still shows Rishab's celebration.

The door creaks open. Everyone turns. Stephano walks in. He moves straight to Flavio's table, drops the bundle of coins and notes in front of him.

FLAVIO

(counting)

"Twenty-five euros. Fine."

FLAVIO

(pauses, grins coldly and continues)

"If your one-legged hero wins the MotoGP

Championship... I'll give you a hundred times this.

But if he doesn't — you never step foot in here again."

STEPHANO
(unflinching)
"I'm game."

THE ROYAL HOTEL – LONDON – RISHAB'S ROOM – NIGHT

The room is dimly lit. The glow of a laptop screen reflects off Rishab and Bharadwaj's focused faces. They're locked in, replaying the qualifier footage — over and over — zeroing in on the left corner sequences.

BHARADWAJ
"We've tested both the qualifying line and the overtaking
line through that left bend... and neither's delivering
results. I've got a new plan. We commit to the racing line
— fast in, fast out. Every corner, especially that left. And
one more thing — your throttle control. If you can feather
the brake while smoothly rolling the throttle... then punch
full gas right at the exit — that burst of acceleration could
be your weapon. That's where you take the lead."

RISHAB
(quietly, almost to himself)
"I hope it works..."

He leans back, exhausted. The weight of what lies ahead pressing down on him. He lies on the bed.

One more race. One final push toward the dream.

RISHAB'S ROOM – LATE NIGHT

Rishab jolts awake — drenched in sweat, chest heaving. A haunting dream of him crashing in the final race.

The fall. The silence. The devastation.

He sits up, runs his hand through his hair and reaches for the phone.

DIAL TONE.

SUJATHA

"Son..."

RISHAB

(voice trembling)

"Maa... I'm scared. I don't know if I'll be able to race tomorrow. I... I need your prayers."

A pause. Then, her voice — calm, warm, unwavering.

SUJATHA

"Rishab... you've come this far on your own grit, your sweat, your fight. I believe in you — more than anyone ever could."

Rishab is silent, holding back tears.

SUJATHA (CONT'D)

"Tomorrow, I'll be watching you, like the whole country. And I'll be watching my son become a world champion. Be fearless !!!"

Her words hit him like lightning. His fear begins to melt — replaced by something deeper.

RISHAB

(smiling through emotion)

"Thank you, Maa..."

@ SILVERSTONE PARK – MORNING

The grandstands tremble with energy. The 12 racers line up, machines roaring like caged beasts. The world watches, millions glued to their screens.

And then a roar from the crowd!!

Rishab walks toward the grid. His prosthetic leg visible, each step defiant. The world doesn't just see a racer — they see a fighter.

Cheers erupt. Flags wave. Flashbulbs go off. Rishab soaks it in — calm and steady.

@ FLAVIO'S PUB – ITALY

The gamblers gather in silence. Beers in hand. Faces tense. Flavio leans forward, eyes narrowed.

Stephano sits in the back calm, eyes locked on the screen. He's not watching a race. He's watching a reckoning.

@ KARUNYA

Sujatha, Chethana, Cpt. Mukherjee and the inmates huddle around a small TV. Rocket sits in the front row, tail wagging.

@ THE COLONY

Salim and the people from the colony have set up a projector to witness their dear friend's race. Firecrackers ready. Eyes wide with hope.

SILVERSTONE PARK – NEAR THE GRID

Bharadwaj walks up to Rishab. This is their final conversation before history decides their fate.

BHARADWAJ

"That left corner...it's still the wall between you and the trophy. But I'll keep believing — like I always have."

RISHAB

(grinning, heart full)

"No fear in my veins today, only the thrill, the wind, the joy of the ride. I'm racing with my soul wide open."

BHARADWAJ

"Then go own the moment, champ !!"

He pulls Rishab in for a tight hug and walks away toward the pit. Rishab stands in front of his bike — his partner in war, his beast, his lifeline.

He gently kneels, places a kiss on the wind shield of the motorcycle.

RISHAB
(whispering to his motorcycle)
"Let's rock."

SILVERSTONE CIRCUIT – THE FINAL RACE!!

The tension is palpable. Cameras flash. Engines hum like growling beasts.

Alessandro walks down to the grid, dragging his motorcycle, calm and commanding. The moment he appears, the grandstands explode in applause and cheers. Fans wave flags, chanting his name — the reigning king has arrived.

All twelve riders take their position. Rishab lines up at 12th — dead last.

The race is 23 laps long. One chance. One title.

The engines roar louder. Throttle grips tighten. Hearts pound.

The hooter blares and they're off.

LAP 1

Alessandro surges ahead like a bullet. The pack follows. Rishab trails — last place, struggling. He wobbles at every left corner, his weakness still haunting him. The JMC pit is silent, eyes grim.

LAPS 2 TO 5

Rishab begins to push. Bit by bit, he picks up speed — but he's still in last. The JMC crew exchanges worried glances.

BHARADWAJ
"Come on, Rishab... not like this..."

LAP 6

Suddenly — **momentum.** Rishab charges forward, overtaking two riders. Now in 9th **position**. The crowd starts noticing.

LAP 7

Rishab hits the left corner — fast in, fast out. The strategy is kicking in. He cuts through the inside. **Now in 5**th.

COMMENTATOR

"That's textbook racing! The left corner... he's mastered it!"

The JMC pit **erupts** — hope is alive.

LAPS 8 TO 14

Rishab holds strong at 5th. His throttle control is flawless. His speed relentless. Alessandro and Martin battle up front — neck and neck, wheel to wheel.

LAP 15

Rishab dives in, overtakes two more riders — now in **3**rd **place**.

The crowd goes wild. The circuit shakes.

LAP 16

Martin edges up to Alessandro — inches apart.

At the right turn, Alessandro cuts in aggressively — a shove. Martin loses control, skids across the track. His bike slams into the barricade.

Rishab dodges, barely inches from disaster. The crowd gasps, then cheers thunderously for Rishab's reflexes.

Martin crawls off the track, fuming, punching the ground.

He's out.

LAP 17

Rishab is now second, tailing Alessandro.

The two riders — **champion vs challenger** are locked in a duel.

They blaze into the left corner.

Alessandro tries the same dirty move — pushes in. Rishab backs slightly, loses momentum. Alessandro pulls ahead.

LAPS 18 TO 20

Alessandro repeats the tactic, squeezing Rishab into the tightest line at the left corners, but Rishab hangs on — just seconds behind. Every inch of the track is war. The crowd is on its feet.

LAP 21

The final laps begin. The camera zooms in on Rishab's visor — his eyes are burning with focus.

LAP 23 – FINAL LAP

The roar is deafening. Rishab and Alessandro — side by side. The entire world is watching.

The final left corner approaches — the one that has haunted Rishab since the beginning. From inside his helmet, Rishab screams:

RISHAB

"This is for you, Maa!!!"

Alessandro shifts — trying to close in on him once again. But this time, Rishab doesn't flinch. He leans hard into the corner, plants his prosthetic knee, and straightens out with a perfect roll-on throttle. He blasts forward.

TRACKSIDE – GRAND STANDS – PIT LANE

The JMC team is on the barricades, screaming.

BHARADWAJ

"GO, RISHAB! GO!"

FINISHING STRAIGHT

Alessandro punches his throttle in desperation. But Rishab is gone — flying like lightning.

He crosses the finish line FIRST !!!

SILENCE. THEN — EXPLOSION OF SOUND.

The crowd erupts.

RISHAB! RISHAB! RISHAB!

Flags wave. Fireworks fire. The JMC crew storms the track. Bharadwaj runs up and lifts Rishab off the bike.

@ FLAVIO'S PUB – ITALY

Pin-drop silence. Faces frozen, however Stephano grins through teary eyes.

@ KARUNYA HOME

Sujatha clasps her hands to her mouth — sobbing with joy. Chethana jumps in joy and embraces Sujatha. The entire home is chanting his name.

Rocket barks wildly in celebration.

@ Salim's Colony

The people erupt in joy while Salim and his friends burst crackers and celebrate Rishab's win.

SILVERSTONE – PODIUM CEREMONY

Rishab stands atop the podium. The national anthem plays. The world watches.

A prosthetic leg. A gold trophy. A teardrop down his cheek.

@ SAIRA'S HOME - LONDON.

Saira sits motionless on the sofa, eyes fixed on the television. Rishab stands on the podium — victorious, radiant, unstoppable.

Tears stream down her face — not of joy, but of remorse. Tears of repentance, of what was lost and of what could never be undone.

She presses her hand to her mouth, trembling. Her eyes whisper the words her lips cannot.

@ JMC HEADQUARTERS – JAPAN

Haruto Ki, seated alone in his sleek glass office, watches the celebration unfold on a massive screen.

Rishab lifts the trophy. Haruto Ki smiles — deeply, proudly.

HARUTO KI

(Murmuring to himself, with quiet conviction)

"I knew it... I knew he was going to make history."

AFTER A MONTH:

MIL – RISHAB'S CABIN – MORNING

Rishab enters the office, calm and composed, still carrying the quiet glow of victory. He steps into his cabin and notices a small stack of envelopes on his desk.

He flips through them absently — until one stops him cold.

It's from Italy. Curious, he tears open the envelope.

Inside is a photograph.

A young man sitting on a motorcycle fitted with support wheels, both legs replaced with prosthetics.

Beside him stands an older man — Stephano — beaming with pride, eyes filled with something more than joy.

Rishab turns the photo over. In bold, heartfelt letters:

THANK YOU, RISHAB.

— With love, Mario & Stephano

Rishab exhales slowly. A smile tugs at his lips. He places the photo gently on his table, as if it were made of glass.

He pulls out a small velvet box from his pocket and opens it gently. Inside — a diamond ring, glinting softly in the morning light. His heart pounds.

Then — a knock on the door. He looks up.

It's Chethana. She stands at the threshold, smiling.

CHETHANA

"May I come in, Champ?"

Rishab's eyes light up. A different kind of victory this time. He rises, his smile warm — vulnerable.

RISHAB

(voice trembling with emotion)

"This feeling... it's lived in my heart for so long, grown with every beat. And now... I just can't hold it in anymore."

He steps toward her, eyes locked with hers. Slowly, he drops to one knee, revealing the ring, his voice soft but steady.

RISHAB (CONT'D)

"Chethana... Will you marry me?"

Chethana gasps, overwhelmed. Tears spill down her cheeks as she falls into his arms, hugging him tightly.

They kiss — a kiss not just of love, but of everything they've survived.

www.ingramcontent.com/pod-product-compliance
Lightning Source LLC
Chambersburg PA
CBHW031040160726
47991CB00005B/1969